She tried to tell herself her mind was playing tricks on her.

A man sat at a polished table with her daughter. He was dressed in faded jeans, a denim shirt—he had the build of a prizefighter, all sinewy muscle.

And yet she could not deny his resemblance to the man she had loved so many years ago....

He glanced up, and his eyes met hers.

The exact color of the little girl's who sat across from him.

This was a dream. No, a nightmare! Her daughter was sitting across the table from the man who bore such a frightening resemblance to the man who had fathered her.

Jordan let the shock of it wash over her. The man who had loved her was a prince. A living, breathing, gorgeous prince.

Dear Reader,

We have some incredibly fun and romantic Silhouette Romance titles for you this July. But as excited as we are about them, we also want to hear from *you!* Drop us a note—or visit www.eHarlequin.com—and tell us which stories you enjoyed the most, and what you'd like to see from us in the future.

We know you love emotion-packed romances, so don't miss Cara Colter's CROWN AND GLORY cross-line series installment, *Her Royal Husband.* Jordan Ashbury had no idea the man who'd fathered her child was a prince—until she reported for duty at his palace! Carla Cassidy spins an enchanting yarn in *More Than Meets the Eye*, the first of our A TALE OF THE SEA, the must-read Silhouette Romance miniseries about four very special siblings.

The temperature's rising not just outdoors, but also in Susan Meier's *Married in the Morning.* If the ring on her finger and the Vegas hotel room were any clue, Gina Martin was now the wife of Gerrick Green! Then jump into Lilian Darcy's tender *Pregnant and Protected,* about a fiery heiress who falls for her bodyguard....

Rounding out the month, Gail Martin crafts a fun, lighthearted tale about two former high school enemies in *Let's Pretend....* And we're especially delighted to welcome new author Betsy Eliot's *The Brain & the Beauty*, about a young mother who braves a grumpy recluse in his dark tower.

Happy reading—and please keep in touch!

Mary-Theresa Hussey

Mary-Theresa Hussey
Senior Editor

Please address questions and book requests to:
Silhouette Reader Service
U.S.: 3010 Walden Ave., P.O. Box 1325, Buffalo, NY 14269
Canadian: P.O. Box 609, Fort Erie, Ont. L2A 5X3

Her Royal Husband

CARA COLTER

SILHOUETTE *Romance*®

Published by Silhouette Books

America's Publisher of Contemporary Romance

Special thanks and acknowledgment are given to Cara Colter for her contribution to the CROWN AND GLORY series.

To my niece, Courtenay Sarvis, with all my love.

 SILHOUETTE BOOKS

ISBN 0-373-19600-8

HER ROYAL HUSBAND

Copyright © 2002 by Harlequin Books S.A.

Visit Silhouette at www.eHarlequin.com

Printed in U.S.A.

Books by Cara Colter

Silhouette Romance

Dare To Dream #491
Baby in Blue #1161
Husband in Red #1243
*The Cowboy, the Baby and
   the Bride-to-Be* #1319
Truly Daddy #1363
A Bride Worth Waiting For #1388
Weddings Do Come True #1406
A Babe in the Woods #1424
A Royal Marriage #1440
First Time, Forever #1464
*Husband by Inheritance #1532
*The Heiress Takes a Husband #1538
*Wed by a Will #1544
What Child Is This? #1585
Her Royal Husband #1600

**The Wedding Legacy

Silhouette Books

The Coltons
A Hasty Wedding

CARA COLTER

shares ten acres in the wild Kootenay region of British Columbia with the man of her dreams, three children, two horses, a cat with no tail and a golden retriever who answers best to "bad dog." She loves reading, writing and the woods in winter (no bears). She says life's delights include an automatic garage door opener and the skylight over the bed that allows her to see the stars at night.

She also says, "I have not lived a neat and tidy life, and used to envy those who did. Now I see my struggles as having given me a deep appreciation of life, and of love, that I hope I succeed in passing on through the stories that I tell."

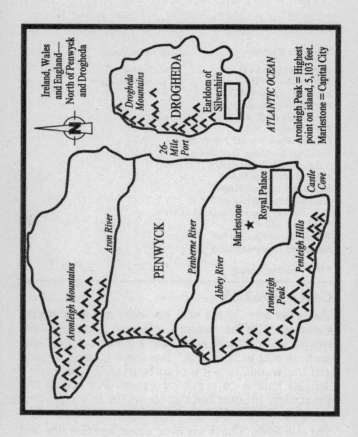

Chapter One

It was the sound he had been waiting for.

The faint rasp of the key in the lock, the tumble of the bolt. Prince Owen Michael Penwyck felt his muscles coiling. He was tense, ready. He became aware he was holding his breath, and blew out slowly, forced himself to breathe.

The heavy wooden door creaked on its ancient hinges. Owen was wedged behind it. He remained focused on the shaft of light that penetrated the darkness of his cell as the door swung slowly open.

A long shadow, elongated, fell across the cold, stone floor. The shadow showed one man, his rifle slung over his shoulder, the sharp angle of his elbow indicating to Owen he carried something in front of him. All was as the young prince had hoped.

The shadow paused, and before he became aware of the broken, empty cot, to register danger, Owen launched himself from behind the door, and smashed into his captor. The man had been carrying a food tray, and some of the contents, steaming soup, a cup of coffee, flipped up onto him and he howled in surprised outrage. And then in pain as Owen pressed the advantage of surprise, and kneed him with all the considerable strength of legs hard-muscled from years of mountain climbing, horseback riding and hiking.

Too much noise, he thought with regret, stepping over the man who had curled up in a fetal position on his cell floor. His captors, alerted by that initial yell, were approaching down the hallway. Owen could hear their footsteps, coming fast, echoing like thunder in the cavernous passage.

Though Owen now knew escape was not likely, not this time, there was fierce swelling within him. It felt like a fire in his breast, a warrior spirit rising. He felt a moment of sweet gratitude for youth and strength, and he unconsciously flexed the hard line of his biceps, filled the breadth of his wide chest with a cleansing breath of air. He took a harder hold on the iron leg he had spent the better part of a day persuading to part company with the cot in his cell.

Fearless, ready, calm, like the knights who had been his ancestors, he stepped out of the doorway. He blinked once, hard, as his eyes adjusted from the murky darkness of the cell to the sudden brightness of the passageway.

Three men were on him almost instantly, dressed in black, faces covered. Owen swung the straight iron bar off the bed, putting all the considerable power of his arm and shoulder into the swing. He felt the jar of connection, and a man toppled to the ground. The bar had glanced off that first man and struck another, and that second attacker backed off warily, swiping at the cut over his eyebrow. He looked at his blood-covered hand with angry, stunned disbelief.

But the third attacker had ducked under the melee of bar and bodies, and was behind Owen. A sinewy arm, appallingly strong, wrapped around the column of the young prince's neck. The second man saw opportunity and rushed forward again. Owen dropped the bed leg and pried ineffectively at the arm that was cutting off his air supply. He reared back, smashing the head of the man who had his arm around his neck with his own head. Though the force stunned him, he was caught in the flow of adrenaline and felt no pain. He heard the other man's grunt, and felt a marginal loosening of the hold on his neck. Owen reared back again, this time kicking forward at the same time. He felt his foot connect with the belly of the second attacker, heard the satisfying ''oomph'' of the air leaving the man. His neck was free.

His satisfaction was short-lived. A black wave of men appeared out of a connecting passageway and was flowing down the hallway toward him.

And the attacker behind him was a demon. He had a clawlike grip on his shoulder now, and was slamming a hard fist over and over into the soft flesh of Owen's cheek. Owen managed to twist, to finally see his opponent head-on.

He was dressed in black, like the others, but the cover had slipped from his face. Even as Owen let loose a punch, and felt the man's nose give under the force of it, he was trying to memorize the hawkish features. He now knew there was no possibility of winning this fight, let alone escaping. Still, some base instinct roared within him, demanded he do as much damage as possible before the inevitable loss.

Owen used the man's own shock against him. He shoved him to the floor, leapt on top of him, his knees bracketing the man's chest. He pulled his arm back, seeing red now, his fury unleashed. But before he could complete his swing, his arm was caught fast and painfully. The air went out of him as someone leapt on his back, shoving him down hard on top of his opponent.

The young prince fought with everything he had left, but there were too many, now, holding him down. One sat on his back, a hard hand on his neck. Both his arms were being held behind him, and hands held his legs. He was lifted enough for the man underneath him to slither out, and then he was slammed back into the cold rock floor.

"Okay," he said, and heard the calm contempt in his own voice, "uncle."

That earned him a hard swat on the back of his head, and he tasted his own blood on his lip. He heard the subtle rattle of metal before he realized what they were doing, and felt his first moment of panic. He fought desperately with his remaining strength, managed to send a man flying and to get his arm free temporarily. But they came back harder than before, and his head was slammed again into the rock floor, and his arm twisted up painfully behind his back. He felt the shackle close and then click shut with cold metallic finality, first around his right wrist and then, despite the wild fury of his struggle, the left one.

More weight settled on him as he tried to writhe away from the leg irons. Cruel hands held him as the iron bands were clamped, too tightly, around his ankles.

He registered, with impotent fury, his own helplessness, and then was jerked roughly to his feet.

He stood, swaying, captured but unsubdued, and then marshaling his remaining strength, he lunged forward. He allowed himself to feel brief satisfaction in the wary respect he saw as men leapt back from him. He noted, too, that for a single, solitary man, he had managed to cause an inordinate amount of damage. The men who faced him were bloody and bruised, their clothing torn and disheveled. His captors' chests were heaving from exertion.

Owen reminded himself he did not have the luxury to gloat. He had only one thing left and he needed to use it. His mind.

Carefully, he looked at the men, taking swift mental notes. They were dressed the same as they had been the night of his kidnapping, in identical black sweatpants, black turtlenecks, now pulled up over the lower part of their faces and black woolen caps. The effect was dramatic and sinister. He tried to get a sense of nationality from the eyes of the men, from their skin color, but he could not. He did get a sense of organization. This was not a motley crew who had decided to capture a prince for ransom.

This was a highly organized group, quasi-military.

He took his eyes from the men. He had been blindfolded when he arrived, and now he looked carefully at the passageway. It looked remarkably like a medieval dungeon, dark and dank. Still, the stones that formed the formidable walls caught his attention. They had a faint pink tinge. His gaze traveled up them. High up the wall was one small opening, barred, no glass. Owen was certain he could smell the sea.

That color of rock was famous on the island of Majorco, an island about to sign a groundbreaking military alliance with Penwyck.

Owen was careful not to let it show in his face that he had a pretty good idea where he was. And maybe even an inkling of why he was being held. There were those who were opposed to this kind of alliance between the two islands.

Maybe more opposed than anyone had ever guessed.

His chance to observe ended abruptly. A boot in his back indicated it was time for him to move back in the direction of his cell. Despite the chains he refused to shuffle, making his stride as long as the chain would allow. He tilted his chin up at a haughty angle.

"Your Royal Highness," one of the men said sarcastically, bowing as he held open the cell door.

Owen slammed his whole body into the man who had been foolish enough to not only mock him, but to take his eyes off of him for a second.

He went down in a hard scrabble of bodies, took another hard punch to his head, and three or four to his rib cage. Then he was picked up and thrown unceremoniously on his cell floor. He watched, panting, his cheek resting on cold stone, as half a dozen of his captors entered the cell, and carried the dismantled bed out, and then the mattress.

The man who had bowed, gave him a kick as he walked by. "You're more like a bloody street fighter than the pampered pouf I was expecting a prince to be," he spat out.

Owen, flattered, managed to laugh through swelling lips, and then became aware of a man standing over him. It was the one whose turtleneck had slipped off his face. He had not bothered to replace it.

He was dabbing at his bloody nose with a handkerchief. Expensive, Owen noted. The eyes that watched him were liquid and black, his lips thin and cruel. Owen memorized the white ridge of the scar that ran from his ear to his jawline.

"A foolish move, Your Highness," the man said

mildly. "Your stay here could have been quite comfortable. Pleasant, even."

From his position on the floor, Owen watched him narrowly. The leader? He listened for an accent. Did he hear a faint Majorcon lilt? Did it mean something that the man was making no attempt to conceal his identity? If it did, what it meant was not good.

"I expect that will be the end of such foolishness," the man said silkily.

Owen said nothing.

The man crouched beside him, balancing on his toes. He rested his arms on his knees and when he did so the right sleeve of his dark tunic pushed up minutely, showing a square of his forearm. Owen tried to look at the unusual tattoo, without appearing to be the least bit interested. Only partially showing, it looked like the tip of a black dagger.

"Is that the end of your foolishness?" the man pressed.

Owen looked deliberately away from the tattoo, met the flat black eyes and said nothing.

The man laughed, a soft, chilling sound. "You are not my prince," he said, "you are my prisoner. When I ask a question of you, I expect an answer."

Educated, Owen decided of his tone, his inflection, his use of words. He answered him by spitting.

He waited for the blow that didn't come.

"The man who guarded you last night said you called out in your sleep." This was said softly, almost kindly.

Owen felt himself go very still. He felt a new wariness. This man was far more dangerous than those who thought they could beat him into submission. He sensed the cutting intelligence, and the ruthlessness of the man.

"You called a name. A name I have not heard before

in connection with your family, not even as a minor player.''

He knows a great deal about my family, Owen noted uneasily. He did not let his unease show.

''Who are you?'' Owen asked, every bit of twenty-three years of royal breeding and training going into the cold authority he inserted into his voice. ''And what do you want?''

The man ignored him, gazed by him thoughtfully. ''What was it now?'' he mused. ''An unusual name.''

Owen was not fooled into believing the man did not know the name.

''Laurie Anne? No, no. Jo Anne, perhaps.''

The man was playing with him, and Owen struggled to look patently bored, even though he dreaded the fact this man might know his deepest secret, or part of it.

''No. Now I recall.'' The gaze was fixed intently on his face, gauging reaction. ''Jordan. That was the name you called in your sleep.''

The black eyes seemed to bore into his own, and Owen knew he had not succeeded in preventing the shock of recognition from flashing in his own eyes even though he had been bracing himself since the moment the man began toying with him.

The man smiled slightly. ''Obviously you are a man who can and will accept the price of personal pain for raising my ire. But will you be responsible for what I would do to others if you push me too far?''

''You would never find her,'' Owen snapped.

''Her,'' his captor said with satisfaction. ''I didn't know that before. Jordan could have been a man's name.''

Owen silently cursed his own stupidity.

''Amazing that someone whose life has been so much

under public scrutiny could have a love interest that no one knows about. I wonder how you managed that? A love interest, is that correct?''

Owen glared silently at his tormentor.

''Do you know there is a drug that will make a man tell everything? His every secret? It's called Sodium Amytal. Have you ever heard of it, Your Royal Highness?''

It was a head game, now, a sparring of minds. Owen was aware if he answered he was conceding to his captor's rules that he was expected to answer him, and that if he didn't answer, the stakes could be upped. *Jordan.* He swallowed his pride.

''No, I haven't heard of that drug,'' Owen said tersely.

''No?'' He nodded slightly acknowledging the younger man's concession. ''Well, princes don't dabble in the dirty stuff, do they? No, they cut ribbons and dance at galas and ride the fall hunt. Though I will admit your strength took me and my men by surprise. But be warned, the drug can make even the strongest man, even a man who can withstand great physical punishment, babble like a baby. I could know everything about your Jordan in very short order.''

''Okay,'' Owen said harshly, ''I hear you.''

''I'm glad that you do.'' The man rose to his feet. ''I think this session is ended for today. Tomorrow I will have some questions. About the diamonds.''

''Diamonds?'' Owen echoed, completely baffled.

''If you give me any more trouble, be warned, I will not punish you. I will find the girl. Do you understand that?''

Owen thought the threat was empty. For one thing, if he made another escape attempt, he fully intended to succeed. But if he did not, how could he tell his captor where Jordan was when he had no idea himself? On the other hand, somewhere in his mind, there were probably clues to her whereabouts. He remembered, uneasily, she was from Wintergreen, Connecticut.

"Do you understand?" he was asked again with soft, but unmistakable menace.

"Yes."

"Good. It's important that we understand each other. Satisfactory answers to the questions I have will also be beneficial to Jordan."

Owen detested himself that he had revealed an Achilles' heel so easily.

"I'll leave your dinner here on the floor where you threw it. If you get hungry enough, it may begin to look appetizing to you, though it's been slightly trampled now. Of course, I am unable to attest to the cleanliness of my men's boots."

Owen struggled with his fresh fury, the abject humiliation of finding himself being totally in this despicable despot's power. He managed to turn over on his side, turn his back to his tormentor.

"Bon appetit, Your Royal Highness."

It was not until he heard the door lock behind him that Owen allowed himself the luxury of a groan.

His whole body was throbbing. Owen would have liked to inspect his knuckles, as it felt like one of them was split open. And touch his face to check the swelling in his cheek, the bleeding from his lip. But his arms were trussed tightly behind his back. He contented himself with laying his hurt cheek against the cold floor.

His bid for freedom had not only failed, it had made the next attempt harder. Perhaps impossible. What if another attempt meant danger to Jordan Ashbury, wherever she was?

The floor seemed harder and colder by the second. Owen steeled his mind to the discomfort, refused to acknowledge the niggle of hunger that had begun in the bottom of his belly.

He had cried her name in the night.

Jordan.

He closed his eyes, and she danced across his memory and came to him. He remembered her running across the sand beside the ocean in the moonlight, her blond hair streaming behind her, the sparkle in her eyes putting the stars to shame. He remembered when he kissed her, that first time, her lips and skin had tasted of the salt in the moist sea air that shrouded them.

The memory made him groan again, a pain deeper than the physical pain he was in.

Because from the start he had known one truth: a relationship with her was impossible.

Impossible.

Impossible to resist. Impossible to control.

And in the end, just plain impossible, his life and hers too far apart, a chasm between worlds too huge to be leaped.

There was rough laughter outside his door. Changing of the guard. He tried to figure out what time it was, but then gave up. Instead, he closed his eyes and gave into the simple pleasure of remembering her speaking his name.

Or what she thought was his name.

He wondered, wearily, if they were going to kill him, these captors. It was the first time he had allowed himself to consider that possible outcome to his kidnapping.

He knew it did not bode well that his captor had allowed him to look at his face, had carelessly revealed the tattoo on his arm.

Looking his mortality in the face, Owen had a moment of illumination, a clarity of thought he had never experienced before.

He was aware, suddenly, that he had let go of the one thing in life that he should have treated as most precious.

He did what he had not allowed himself to do for five years. He allowed himself to remember her. He allowed himself to wish things could have been different.

He had been eighteen the summer of his rebellion.

Eighteen and aware that he was more likely than his twin brother, Dylan, to be chosen to be king one day.

What had it been about being eighteen that had made truths of which he had always been aware seem suddenly unbearable?

He had always known his life would not be his own.

He had always known that every decision regarding his life and every detail affecting his life would be carefully orchestrated, not to meet his needs, but to meet the needs of his small island nation of Penwyck.

He had always known that the most important decisions of *his* life, including whom he would one day marry, would largely be influenced by others.

At eighteen, he had seen his life unfolding before him, a prison he could not escape. He could see now they were grooming him to be king, and not his brother Dylan. He could see how it hurt Dylan, and he had hated a system that would make one brother seem to have more value than another, just because he had different gifts.

Owen was strong and fast and smart. Dylan was those things, too, but not to the same extent. And Dylan had quiet strengths of his own that were largely overlooked because Owen was a "package" that the public adored. Tall, dark and handsome, the fact that he was good-looking and athletic played a part in the manufacture of a fairy tale that the people of Penwyck delighted in believing. Sometimes Owen was uncomfortably aware of his image being manipulated more than Dylan's, his acceptance as the future monarch of the small island being worked on in subtle and not-so-subtle ways all the time.

Most men, Owen knew, had to find their destiny. He had been born to his.

At eighteen, he accepted that. But he also realized he had some trading power. And the trade he insisted on was that he have a summer of freedom—one summer in the United States—before he came back and devoted himself and his life totally to the destiny he had been born to. In exchange for one summer he promised he would return to Penwyck without argument and ready and willing to assume his adult role in the affairs of state.

Even with that promise, he had to fight hard. It was the first time he came face-to-face with the implacable strength of his own warrior spirit.

He found it to be a part of himself that he enjoyed thoroughly.

Disguised, drilled in his assumed identity until he could recite it in his sleep, under oath not to reveal his true self to anyone, under any circumstances, Owen was finally allowed, albeit reluctantly by his parents, and especially by the Royal Elite Team, to go off completely on his own for what was supposed to be a five week program for gifted political science students at the world-renowned Smedley Institute at Laguna Beach in California.

"Hey, you, blond boy."

Those were the first words she'd said to him, her voice laced with scorn, no doubt because she had realized he was no more a natural blonde than she was a sumo wrestler.

He'd recognized her as the smart girl, the one who was not afraid to raise her hand, who did her homework, who had the answers, who was on the lookout for sexism. She had shoulder-length blond hair and she could have been pretty, if she tried, but he suspected she would have scorned expending energy in such a superficial pursuit.

That day her jeans and T-shirt were way too baggy for her slight figure, and her beautiful eyes were almost hidden by the brim of a ball cap she had pulled down too low.

Almost. Because when he looked in her eyes for the very first time, he had felt a strange shiver. Her eyes were not the eyes of the class brain, nor even the eyes of a woman who could slice a man with her razor wit. Her gaze was calm, and strong, almost unsettling in what it said about her.

Honest. Trustworthy. Kind.

The word *destiny* had formed unbidden in his brain as he looked at her, but how could that be when his was already so rigidly outlined for him and when she so obviously thought men were beer-swilling swine whom she had to guard against at all times?

He'd crossed his arms over his chest, rocked back on his chair and replied, "What can I do for you, blond girl?"

She'd smiled, reluctantly.

"I drew your name on the class project. Ben Prince, right? Despite the movie star jaw and the underwear model body, I expect you to pull your weight."

He'd always been treated with the complete deference of one born to royalty. "Underwear model body?" he'd sputtered with royal indignation. On the other hand, that meant Miss Priss had been looking. He took off the heavy glasses that were part of his disguise. If she was looking, he had a simple male need to look great.

"I know you don't need those," she said. "What are they for? To make you look more intelligent?"

So, she had seen through the Royal Elite Team's best disguise in no time flat. But *look more intelligent*, as if nothing he had contributed in class had convinced her of that? It occurred to him, tangling with her would be about as much fun as tangling with a porcupine.

If you believed her words, believed her eyes, then you knew she was as much in disguise as you were, his inner voice chided.

"Don't worry," she'd said airily. "All I'm worried about is what you have up here," she'd tapped his forehead lightly, "under the Miss Clairol."

"Miss Clairol?" he'd asked, slightly dazed because her touch said things her demeanor did not. Her demeanor said, loudly, ice-cold. Her touch said, even more loudly, red-hot.

"Blonde in a bottle," she'd whispered. "Hair dye."

"I'm disguised," he said coolly.

"Really? FBI's Most Wanted list?"

"Close. Royal family. Small island kingdom you've never heard of."

She'd laughed out loud, caught off guard and unexpectedly delighted, even while he was uncomfortably aware he'd done, jokingly, something he had given his promise not to do. Told her who he was.

Her laughter changed everything. It erased the wariness from her face, and the stiffness from the way she held herself.

"Well, Your Royal Muckety-muck," she'd said,

straight-faced, now, but still relaxed, "which despot in history would you like to do our project on? I thought maybe Stalin."

"Genghis Khan," he said, knowing she wanted to walk all over him, and if he let her, he would never be allowed to explore the deeper mystery of her calm eyes.

"Wow. Are you actually planning on contributing to this? You're not just going to let me do all the work while you go down to the beach and ogle girls in their bikinis?"

"As tempting as that sounds, I'm actually here to learn something."

She looked at him with reluctant respect, and then smiled. Really smiled, no barriers. It won him completely. Not that he let her know that for a good long time. At least a day and a half.

And so it began. Huddled over tables at study hall, grabbing quick hamburgers, throwing ideas back and forth, reworking sentences, drawing time lines.

That's how he'd come to love the way she thought—her wry humor, her quick intelligence, the way she danced with words, how much fun it was to spar with her mind.

That's how he had started to notice the smell of her hair, the light that danced in her eyes, the breathtaking figure she hid under all those layers of clothes she was so fond of.

And he found, just as the first time, he told her over and over who he really was. In ways he had never told another living soul.

That was her gift to him. She allowed him to be normal. To explore normal dreams and ambitions, to be a normal eighteen-year-old guy.

Jokingly, they had called each other Blond Boy and

Blond Girl. She teased him unmercifully when his natural dark brown, nearly black hair began to grow out, giving him roots.

How quickly he had come to see her inner beauty, her sharp mind, her wonderful sense of humor, her huge capacity to be kind.

They had become the best of friends almost instantly. It was a relationship based, originally, on mutual respect for each other's intelligence.

He knew he had to make it stay that way. He knew he could not allow himself to love her. But he sensed he had begun the fall that even the most powerful of men seemed powerless to stop.

Unless he was mistaken Owen Michael Penwyck, aka Ben Prince, was falling in love with Jordan Ashbury.

Without the press looking on, without a royal council vetting his choice, without her lineage being subjected to scathing scrutiny.

He was just a normal guy with a normal girl who had been given the gift of an extraordinary summer.

Respect deepened to admiration, words deepened to silence, eyes locking deepened to hands holding, liking deepened to love. Just like that.

Now, lying in a cell, contemplating the possibility his life was over, and thinking with a clarity that seemed illuminated from the heavens, Owen acknowledged his regret. His one mistake.

Unable to leave her at first, he had begged for and been given an extension on his stay. Two more weeks of exploring remote beaches, and remote places of the heart. Two more weeks of her hand in his, her lips on his eyelids, his hands allowed to go where no man's had gone before his. But when that was gone, he had phoned home and begged again. This time he had been refused, so he had done what any eighteen-year-old boy in the throes of first passion would have done. He had refused to go home, and moved into Jordan's tiny basement suite off campus.

He remembered the last night, when he could feel it coming to an end, knew his days were numbered.

"Tell me one thing about you that no one else in the world knows," he had begged. "Your deepest secret." Something of her that he could hold onto forever.

They had been in her tiny bed. Was there anything more wonderful than two people in a single bed? With her naked skin against him, and her hair, soft and fine as a baby's spread over his chest, with her fingers tangled in his, she told him.

"I'm a closet romance nut."

"What?"

"I know. Under all that sarcasm and biting intelligence that scares the boys away, I was dying to be loved, Ben Prince. Dying. Underneath my bed at home are three full boxes of romance novels. Historicals are my favorite."

He had tightened his hold on her, kissed her temple, knew what she was really telling him was that she had been lonely. And he felt sick that she would be lonely again, soon.

She sighed against him. "It's like two people live inside of me. The one who wants to be the first female mayor of Wintergreen, Connecticut. And the one who would love to be riding through the dark woods in a carriage, when from their mysterious depths comes a highwayman."

They had made love after that, wild, passionate, completely unbridled.

"Thank you for making me so happy," she had said

sleepily, trustingly. And he had lain awake, knowing he had to tell her the truth about himself, and knowing at the same time he could not.

In the morning, he had gotten up before her. He walked down to their favorite oceanfront café to get her a croissant and one of those specialty coffees she adored. Filled with thoughts of waking her up with his lips on her cheek, he had walked into a trap.

Four members of the Royal Elite Team, apparently tipped off about his routine, were waiting for him there. They had been sent to escort him home. No more extensions.

"I just need to do one thing. Alone. I promise I'll come right back. One hour."

"We can escort you where you need to go, sir."

But then they would know about her, and her life would be scrutinized and investigated and torn apart for no reason. The security team was the best, but what if there was a leak? What if the tabloids went after her?

"No, no escort." He must have looked like he was going to make a dash for it, because he'd found himself in the center of a circle of big, intimidating men, who looked sympathetic but unmoving.

"Sir, please don't make us do this the hard way."

No goodbyes and no explanations. Maybe it was better that way. Maybe it would be better if she hated him, rather than held some hope in her heart.

He had made a vow, and he was now being asked to keep it.

Owen turned his back on that part of his life that would have made him insane had he allowed himself to dwell on it, to remember it.

He returned to Penwyck and threw himself into the

role he had been born to play, the role he had agreed to play in exchange for one magical summer.

He tirelessly attended functions, raised funds for charities and worked on economic development projects for his country. He felt the adoration of the people and tried to be worthy of it. When the Penberne River did its annual flood, Prince Owen was filling sandbags, shoulder to shoulder with the citizens of Sterling. When the Lad and Lassies Clubs were having a fund-raiser he could be counted on to take a turn in the dunking booth, to buy the first pie at the raffle. He cut ribbons and gave speeches, danced the first dance of each and every charity ball.

The rift between he and his brother deepened—Dylan not understanding his brother wasn't trying to win a crown—he was trying to outrun a broken heart.

It was only his mother that he knew he had failed to convince. Sometimes he caught her watching him, unveiled sadness in her eyes. But had he not always detected a faint sadness when his mother looked at him?

A sadness that was not present in her eyes when she looked at Dylan?

Even so, he knew it to be intensified now.

And really, his campaign who was leading him down the road to being king, and away from the road of being normal, had almost worked.

Had worked until the precise moment his bedroom door had blasted open in the middle of the night, a drug-saturated cloth had been forced over his face, and he had been kidnapped.

Now, ironically, in a cell where the prince had nothing, he had everything once more.

Her memory came to him. And brought him comfort.

Once again he could smell her and taste the salt on her lips, feel the silk of her hair sliding through his hands.

"If I die," he mumbled, "I will die happy if my last thoughts are of her."

She filled him, and he felt content.

He almost didn't want to be drawn back from where he was by the far off sound that he could have mistaken for firecrackers, had he not been waiting for it.

Gunfire. It could only mean a rescue attempt.

And he knew he had to do his part. He struggled back from Jordan's memory, and yet it filled him with a strength such as he had never known.

Shackled, he lurched to his feet. When his cell door flew open, and it was the enemy who arrived first, he lowered his head, like a battering ram, and charged.

And held them until he saw the familiar crest of Penwyck's Royal Navy Seals on the dark clothed men now swarming down the hall, the enemy fleeing in front of them.

"Your Royal Highness," a man said, stepping toward him, his smile white against the camo-darkened skin of his face.

Owen recognized the voice and took a closer look. It was his cousin, Gage Weston, a man who had made a calling of showing up where there was trouble.

Gage said, "With all due respect, you fight like a man who was born to it."

Owen smiled wearily. "So I've been told."

He looked back at his cell, and felt relief. Jordan would be safe now. All his secrets were safe.

Except for the one he had been keeping from himself. He had never, ever stopped loving her.

Chapter Two

Jordan Ashbury woke partially, her heart beating frantically within her chest.

So real was the feeling that his kiss was on her lips, that she ran her tongue along them, hoping the faint taste of salted sea air would be lingering there. When it was not, she reached across the tangle of her sheets, wanting to be reassured by the silky touch of his skin under her fingertips, wanting the ache within her to be eased by his presence in her bed.

When her fingertips touched cold emptiness, Jordan came fully awake and smelled the mingled aroma of wood smoke and fall leaves coming in her open window, not the sea. Her sheets were covered in a prim pattern of yellow teacup roses. They were sheets that had never known the skin of a man.

The ache was there, though, as real as if it had been yesterday, instead of just over five years ago, that she had awoken and he had been gone. For good. Forever. Without so much as a goodbye.

He had warned her it would be that way. The warning had not made it one bit easier to cope with when it had happened.

Jordan shook herself fully awake, angry. She sat up and fluffed her pillow with furious punches. She glanced at her bedroom clock. It was only three-thirty in the morning. She clenched her eyes tight, commanded herself back to sleep.

She had not had one of those dreams for so long. It had been at least six months. She thought that meant her heart was mending, finally.

She would not go as far as to say she was happy. Jordan Ashbury mistrusted happiness. It was the crest of an exhilarating wave you rode before it tossed you carelessly onto sharp and jagged rocks.

But she would say she was content. She had her girls—the young, unwed mothers she did volunteer work with. She had her job with her aunt. She had this little humble house she had just purchased. And of course, she had Whitney, her four-year-old daughter, who had enough exuberance for both of them.

And she had the new male in her life. There he was now. He prowled into her bedroom, leapt onto the bed in a single graceful leap, curled up by her ear and began to purr.

Jay-Jay, named in honor of Jason, whom she had dated once and hated, and Justin whom she had dated twice and liked. Both had been dismissed from her life with equal rapidity.

"No time," she'd told her mother who had set up both disasters.

"But aren't you lonely?" her mother wailed.

"Of course not," she had said, strong and breezy.

"It's a brand-new world, Mom. Women don't need men to feel they have purpose, to feel complete."

"Working with those unwed mothers is making you cynical about men," her mother said.

No, it wasn't. It was reminding her, over and over, of the life lesson she most needed reminding of.

Love hurt.

Well, not Whitney love. Not Mom and Dad love. Not Jay-Jay love. Just the other kind. Man-woman love.

Only in the middle of the night, like this, did the insanity of loneliness take her, try to pull her down, make her wistful, make her ache with yearning.

"Weak ninny," she scolded herself, opened her clenched eyes to glance at the clock then closed them again with renewed determination. Sleep.

Instead, a chill washed over Jordan, a chill not caused by the cool September air sliding through her open window. In that space between wakefulness and sleep where her mind sometimes shook free of her tight hold on the reins, she allowed herself to wonder, did it mean something that she had dreamed of Ben?

Why did she feel a knot in her stomach, a shadow in her soul? Was he in trouble? Was he dead?

She shivered, caught in the grip of something that felt weirdly like premonition.

Ben Prince did not exist, she reminded herself bitterly. How could he be dead when he had never been alive?

Except he was alive, amazingly so, in the sapphire-blue eyes of their daughter. Her daughter. The child he knew nothing about.

Jordan had tried to tell him. It seemed the only thing, the decent thing. That was when she'd found out, through the registrar's office at the Smedley Institute where they had met during a summer program, there was no Ben Prince.

Short of yelling at them that a figment of her imagination could not have produced a pregnancy, there was nothing more she could do. He was gone.

Except in that place where her dreams took her.

Restless, she got out of bed, went over and slammed the window shut. She paused and looked out at Maple Street, Wintergreen, Connecticut. This was not the best area of town, but it was old, so the maple trees were enormous, just beginning to hint at their fall splendor. The houses that lined the street were tiny, asphalt-shingled boxes, but the yards were generous, which is what she had wanted for Whitney.

When she was growing up, Jordan had always assumed she would end up in a neighborhood like her parents, spacious Dutch colonial and Cape Cod homes set well back from the road, sporting wraparound verandas and porch swings and lawn chairs where people whiled away hot summer nights.

A perfect all-American street in a perfect all-American neighborhood. The scent of apple pies baking wafted out the windows at this time of year, and red, white and blue flags flew from porch pillars.

Of course, she had spoiled her parents' all-American dreams for her by showing up pregnant, no marriage, no man.

Forgiveness had been some time coming though Whitney's entrance into the universe seemed to have greased the wheels of progress considerably.

Her parents had objected to Jordan buying her own little house six months ago. Of course, it made more sense for her to continue living with them. She was a single mom with a limited income. Her options, which had once seemed endless, now seemed limited.

Even so, she liked her life. Was contented with it. Ninety percent of the time.

Still, looking at that quiet street, washed in silver moonlight, Jordan felt restless. What had happened to the girl who beamed out of her senior high yearbook, the banner Most Likely To Succeed draped across the picture?

Once upon a time, not so very long ago, she had been politically ambitious, certain she would be the first female mayor of Wintergreen.

It was that ambition that had made her sign up for an intense political science summer program at Laguna Beach the summer after her graduation from high school.

It had turned out to be her date with destiny—and she was not sure yet that she had recovered from the surprise that her destiny was not even close to what she had planned for herself.

Now, she was a chef's assistant working for her aunt. It was a job Jordan had fallen into, rather than planned for. Given that, it was surprisingly satisfactory.

She no longer had any desire to be mayor. She just wanted to be a good mom to her small firebrand of a daughter. She wanted to help other girls, who like herself, found themselves thrown up on love's rocks, battered and bruised. Priorities changed that quickly.

Reminding herself sternly she had to work tomorrow, she climbed back into bed, and tossed restlessly until the phone jangled shrilly. Startled, Jordan looked at her bedside clock—6:00 a.m. No one in their right mind called that early in the morning. It must be Marcella. She was due the third week of September.

"Hello?" she answered, already pulling on her jeans.

She could drop off Whitney at her parents, call Meg, be in the labor room in fifteen minutes.

"Jordan, you are not going to believe this!"

She sat down on the edge of her bed, and eased the jeans back off. "I'm already having trouble with belief. Aunt Meg, when have you ever been up at this time of the morning?"

"Never," her aunt admitted. "But it was worth it! Did I wake you? Never mind. You'll think it's worth it, too."

"We've been hired to cater the presidential ball?" Jordan asked, tongue-in-cheek.

"Better. It's because of the time zone difference that they called so early."

Better than the presidential ball? Jordan was intrigued despite herself. "Aunt Meg, who called so early?"

"Lady Gwendolyn Corbin, lady-in-waiting to Queen Marissa Penwyck of the island kingdom of Penwyck."

Jordan, confused, checked her calendar. As she thought, it was still September, not anywhere near April Fool's day. She sighed. Her lovely aunt, a chef extraordinaire, always walked the fine line between genius and eccentricity. Sadly, she had obviously finally crossed the line.

"Jordan, listen! She wants me—us—to cater the party. At the palace! Right there on the island of Penwyck! We get to go there, all expenses paid. Oh my, Jordan, it is the break I've been waiting for. I told you that little piece in *Up and Coming People* was going to do it. I told you!"

The article in the national magazine *Up and Coming* had been dreadful. It had made her aunt seem considerably more eccentric than she was, which must have been a stretch for the writer. It had featured Meg's experiments combining edible flowers with pastry. "Flaky Flowers" had been the title of the piece and it had gone downhill from there.

"Aunt Meg, slow down," she suggested gently, suspecting the article had generated a prank. "Where have you been asked to go? And what have you been asked to do?"

Her aunt took a deep breath. "You read about it in the papers, didn't you? Or saw it on television?"

"Flaky Flowers was on television?" Jordan asked, appalled that her aunt might have been held up for ridicule at a new and dizzying level.

"Not Flaky Flowers. Jordan, the whole world has been talking about nothing else. You missed it, didn't you?" This was said with undisguised accusation.

"I suppose I might have," Jordan admitted uncertainly.

Her aunt sighed. "You are taking this heartbroken recluse thing to radical limits."

"I prefer to think of myself as a strong, independent woman," Jordan said, miffed. She could feel a headache coming on. She did not feel prepared to defend her lifestyle choices at six in the morning.

"Same thing," her aunt said.

"What world event did I miss?" she asked, trying to get her aunt back to the point and away from her personal life.

"The kidnapping of that prince! And now he's been safely returned to his home and his mother, *the queen,* is having a party to celebrate, and I'm catering and you're coming with me!"

I hope this isn't real, Jordan thought. "Is this real?"

"Of course. A celebration for those closest to the family. Which is a mere one hundred and seventy-five. Dinner, of course before the ball. Did you hear me, Jordan? A ball, like in Cinderella.''

The fairy tale Jordan most alluded to when she told frightened young expectant mothers not to believe in fairy tales. The prince was not coming to rescue them. Sometimes, Jordan even found herself wishing the story could have a different ending, but it rarely did.

''A midnight snack will be necessary,'' her aunt went on, not intercepting the chilly response to Cinderella. ''What do you think? My Moose Ta-Ta for the main course?''

Despite the name, Meg's Moose Ta-Ta was to die for: roast beef done in a secret sauce that Meg claimed included the unshed velvet of a moose antler.

When she debated saying it might be hard to procure that much velvet, Jordan realized she was being sucked into the incredible vortex of her aunt's enthusiasm. ''I can't help you, Aunt Meg.''

''What?!'' This said in the same tone Cruella used when she was refused the puppies.

''No,'' Jordan said firmly, ''I can't possibly. I told you from the beginning I wouldn't travel. Couldn't. I am giving my daughter stability.''

''What you are giving your daughter is a boring life. Boring. Boring. Boring.''

''Plus, Marcella's baby is due any day. I can't just leave her in the lurch.''

''Jordan, which member of your group had her baby last? Stacey? You had nine people in the delivery room with her. That's a baseball team. You don't need to be there.''

''The girls like knowing I'm there for them.'' Like no one else ever has been.

"I think you should find a volunteer activity that doesn't underscore your anger at men."

Menu discussion to free psychology advice from the woman who had proudly named Moose Ta-Ta. Jordan noted her headache seemed to be intensifying, moving around from the center of her forehead toward her ears.

"I like my boring life, and my volunteer work," Jordan said, a touch testily. She had experienced the other. She had experienced exhilaration. Magic. Wonder. It was exhausting. The pain of losing those kinds of things never dulled, ever.

Boring on the other hand was nice and dull to begin with. It was hard to go downhill from there.

"Of course you adore boring, dear," her aunt said soothingly, "but you must come. You must. As a teensy-weensy favor to your favorite aunt who can no longer survive without you. Who else could I trust with the icing for the Dancing Chocolate Ecstasy?"

"I won't leave my daughter and Marcella in order to baby-sit your active bacterial cultures."

"Darling, you never even let me get to the best part! Whitney can come. They've given me a blank check. Me and my entire entourage are expected in Penwyck by tomorrow evening. Lady Gwendolyn used that word. Entourage. I mentioned Whitney, of course. I knew I wouldn't be able to pry you away from her. They'll provide a nanny!"

"I can't," Jordan said, sensing a danger she did not understand. "That kind of trip sounds like it would be terribly unsettling to a small child. Too whirlwind. Too exotic. Too chaotic. Too...you know."

"No. You know. Me. And I am not taking no for an answer. I will come right over there and tell Whitney her deranged mother has refused an all-expense-paid trip for two to an island with a real castle, a real king and queen, real princesses, and two real princes.''

''Don't you dare! She'll—''

''—torment you until you agree to go,'' Aunt Meg said with satisfaction. ''Don't make me do it, Jordan. Just say yes to the adventure, for once!''

''I said yes to an adventure, once,'' Jordan reminded her aunt stiffly.

''And you have a lovely daughter to show for it. Besides, I'll pay you double, plus a very generous living out allowance. Aren't you saving for a microwave for that little meeting room of yours? So you can serve nice, healthy soup to all your young moms-to-be? I'll even donate soup.''

Sometimes there was just no arguing with Meg. Besides, Marcella did have a good support network. Her mom and her sister were both very supportive of her, and both had already expressed an interest in being there for the delivery.

Suddenly, without warning, that yearning came over Jordan. To say yes to adventure even though the price could be so high. Wasn't it worth it?

Just by closing her eyes she could still remember how it felt, those seven weeks in July when her soul had been on fire.

''All right,'' she said slowly, giving into the impulse, the yearning, ''All right. I'll come.''

Her aunt whooped so loudly into the phone that she nearly deafened her poor niece. After hearing what needed to be done, and in very short order, Jordan hung up the phone and looked at it bemused.

''Why do I have the awful feeling I'm going to regret this?'' she asked herself. And yet, if she was honest, regret was not what she felt.

She felt the tiniest stirring of excitement, a feeling she had not allowed herself to have, not in this way, since a morning five years ago when she had woken up to the cold, hard reality of a bed empty beside her, and the terrifying knowledge she was now totally alone with the secret of the baby growing inside of her.

"Meg," Jordan told her aunt, "no nasturtiums. I cannot find a fresh nasturtium on all of Penwyck."

"Oh," her aunt wailed, "the pastry just doesn't have the same flavor with geranium leaves. See what it would cost to import some. Orange. I only want orange ones. No yellow."

Jordan stared at her aunt, and allowed herself to feel exhausted. They'd arrived here in Penwyck less than twenty-four hours ago. Jet-lagged, arriving practically in the middle of the night, Jordan had not really noticed much about the island as they were whisked to the castle, and into quarters that adjoined the banquet kitchen. The quarters were motel room plain and seemed distinctly humble and uncastlelike.

The nanny, Trisha, had been introduced to her early the following morning. A teenage girl, she was an absolute doll. With those shifting loyalties young children are so famous for, Whitney had given her heart to the young girl completely and irrevocably and only stopped by on brief visits to the kitchen to tell her mother she had seen "a weel thwone with weel jewels" or "a weel pwincess with a weel pwetty smile."

Jordan, on the other hand, had seen only her quarters, the kitchen and the small office off of it, which housed a cranky telephone that was like nothing she had ever seen in America. She was developing a healthy hatred for the instrument and dreaded trying to call overseas now in the never ending search for nasturtiums.

She'd been going flat-out, putting out fires, soothing her ruffled aunt, trying to find impossible ingredients and, of course, nursing that active yogurt culture, the secret ingredient that made her aunt's Dancing Chocolate Ecstasy so unbelievably delicious.

She was exhausted. "Only orange nasturtiums," she repeated, turning from her aunt.

"Miss Jordan! Miss Jordan!"

Her relief at being called from her quest for orange nasturtiums was short-lived. Trisha was rushing across the kitchen toward her, obviously close to tears.

"I've lost her," she wailed. "Miss Jordan, I've lost Whitney."

For the first time since they had arrived, Jordan allowed herself to wish she had listened to her doubts.

"I knew I was going to regret this," she said. "I just knew it."

"Jordan, don't overreact," Meg said, bustling by, her hands full of something that looked dangerously like the moss that crept up the castle walls. "Whitney has gone exploring. Perfectly normal for a child that age. She's having fun. You know, maybe a few yellow would be all right."

"My daughter is missing, and she's four years old. Excuse me if I give that priority over yellow nasturtiums."

Meg gave her a hurt look, put the moss in a large pot and turned her back on her.

"One minute she was there, ma'am," the young nanny said tearfully, "and the next she simply wasn't. I've looked everywhere."

"How long have you been looking?" Jordan asked

firmly, though she would have liked dearly to wring her hands and cry just like the nanny.

"Nearly an hour."

An hour. In an enormous castle, full of hazards, coats of armor waiting to be pulled down, swords waiting to impale. And what of all the strange people? The prince had been kidnapped from this very castle only two weeks ago!

Jordan forced herself to take a deep and steadying breath. She whipped off her apron.

Her aunt peered up from the pot she was stirring, which was emitting strange clouds of green steam. "I wish you'd think of the Dancing Chocolate Ecstasy. A mistake at this phase, and it's ruined!"

Jordan glared at her, and turned back to the quivering nanny. "Where were you exactly when you noticed her gone? Take me there."

For the first time, Jordan entered the main part of the castle. Despite her worry for Whitney, she could not help but notice the richness all around her. Thick muted carpets covered stone floors. Richly colored tapestries and stern oil paintings covered the stone walls. The furniture was all antique, glowing beautifully from hours of elbow grease. Intricate crystal chandeliers hung from ceilings. Oak had been used extensively on bannisters and window casings and doorways. All in all, the opulence was somewhat overwhelming.

"We were right here, ma'am," the girl finally said, stopping in a quiet hallway on the second floor. The carpet under their feet looked priceless. A muted tapestry, obviously silk and obviously ancient hung on one wall, a portrait of a fierce-looking man mounted on a horse hung on the opposite wall.

Jordan could see nothing here that would fascinate her daughter.

"I had just paused for a moment, to talk to Ralphie, one of the gardeners, and when I looked at where she had been, Whitney was gone!"

Jordan decided not to pursue what Ralphie-the-gardener might have been doing on the second floor of the palace.

There only seemed to be one place Whitney could have gone. "And this door goes where?" Jordan asked.

"That's Prince Owen's suite, ma'am."

"Did you tell her that? My daughter? That a real live prince resided behind those doors?"

Trisha looked painfully thoughtful. "Well, yes I might have mentioned it."

Jordan pushed down the handle, but the young nanny flung herself in front of her, wide-eyed with disbelief.

"You can't just enter his suite," she whispered.

"My daughter might be in there!"

"Surely not." The girl looked terrified.

"What is the prince? Why are you so afraid? Is he some sort of old ogre?"

A blush crept charmingly up the girl's cheeks. "Oh, no, ma'am. Not in the least. I mean nothing further from an ogre. He's not old for one thing. And he's the most handsome man who ever lived. And so wonderfully kind. He's very, oh, just the best. But you can't just enter his quarters."

So much for Ralphie, Jordan thought, grimly amused by the girl's obvious crush.

"I could never presume to knock on his door," the girl whispered. "If he finds out I've lost a child in my charge, I'll never live with the shame of it. He's going to be king some day!"

"What nonsense," Jordan said, and hammered on the door. Despite the nanny's gasp of dismay, she pushed down the handle before there was an answer. Prince or not her child was lost and royal protocol came a long way down the list from that.

"Excuse me—" she stopped dead in her tracks, and felt the blood drain from her face.

Whitney was there after all, sitting happily at a huge table, manipulating chessmen that appeared to be made of crystal.

But the discovery of her daughter brought none of the expected relief. Instead, Jordan felt close to panic.

She tried to tell herself her mind was playing tricks on her.

Of course it was.

A man sat at a polished table with her daughter. Not the prince, obviously. He was dressed in faded jeans, and a denim shirt with a smudge of dirt on the elbow. He had the build of a prizefighter, all sinewy muscle, and the look of one, too, his face bruised, his lip split. This must be the famous Ralphie-the-gardener. Obviously those distortions to his facial features had momentarily made her think the impossible.

And yet she could not deny his resemblance to the man she had loved so many years ago, when once before she had said yes to adventure.

No, it wasn't him.

Ben had been blond. This man's hair was dark as fresh-turned loam. Besides, he was broader through the shoulders, and the chest than Ben had been. It wasn't him. It couldn't be.

She reminded herself that this happened to her from time to time—a glimpse at a stranger set her heart to beating wildly, filled her with the joyous thought, *it's him,* before she had a chance to remind herself seeing him again would be nothing to be joyous about.

He glanced up. The way his hair, just a touch too long, fell over his brow, made her take a step back, and then his eyes met hers.

Deep, cool, the exact color of sapphires. The exact color of the little girl's who sat across from him.

This was a dream. No, a nightmare, that she imagined her daughter sitting across the table from the man who bore such a frightening resemblance to the man who had fathered her.

But if she could have convinced herself it wasn't him, the look on his face shattered that.

Stunned recognition washed over his features before he scrambled to his feet.

"Leave us," he said to the flustered nanny, sending only the briefest glance her way.

"You do not have to leave us," Jordan snapped. "I'm sure your duties do not include taking instructions from Ralphie-the-gardener."

Trisha looked like she was going to faint. "No ma'am," she whispered, standing like a deer caught in headlights, "but this is not Ralph."

"Leave," he said again, curtly.

The girl actually curtsied, and flushed to a shade of purple that reminded Jordan of the fresh beets lined up for the Blushing Beet Borscht they were preparing in the kitchen.

"Yes, Your Royal Highness," Trisha squeaked, and backed out of the room, tripping over herself in her haste to get out of the door.

Your Royal Highness. Jordan let the shock of it wash over her. The man who had loved her was a prince. A living, breathing, gorgeous prince.

He was still the man who had left her, she reminded herself. That meant he was still a cad.

The silence was electric as she regarded him. She wanted him to flinch away from the fury in her look, but instead she could feel the familiar intensity of his gaze, could feel it threatening to melt in an instant what it had taken her five long hard years to build.

"Hi, Mommy," Whitney said, looking up, breaking the silence.

She saw the shock cross his features.

"Mommy?" he said, almost accusingly, as if he had a right to know what had transpired in her life in the past years—as if he was shocked she had the audacity to have a life without him.

"Your Royal Highness?" she shot back, just as accusingly.

"Pwince Owen," Whitney filled in helpfully.

"Oh my," Jordan said, allowing a faint hint of sarcasm into her voice, "and I thought it was Prince Ben. Or was that Ben Prince?"

"It was Blond Boy, wasn't it?" The faintest twinkle appearing in his eye.

How could he be trying to make this light? She *hated* that twinkle. It was part of his easy charm, his great big lying charming self. There had probably been dozens after her, who felt the very same weakness she had felt when he gazed at her with those amazing passionate seductive eyes.

The bruises, the marks of the beating on his face only added to his pull—the almost irresistible desire to touch him with tender fingertips. Traitor fingers!

"Of course, you feel passionate about him," Jordan would tell those sobbing girls who came to her house late in the night, "that's what got you into this mess in the first place. But there's no need to be a weak ninny about it.''

Here she was, being given an opportunity to practice what she preached. She was not going to forgive the betrayal that had nearly torn her soul from her body five years ago, the betrayal that had turned her from an innocent and idealistic child to a cynical and wounded woman in the blink of an eye, just because he had the most mesmerizing eyes of any male on the planet.

''Well, Your Royal—'' she hesitated, tempted to call him Your Royal Muck-muck, to show his title did not impress her in the least, did not make up for his great failings in character, but she thought he might think she was playfully referring to their shared past, so she bit her tongue and called him Highness. ''I guess your identity explains a great deal, up to and including this dream contract of my aunt's.''

''Jordan,'' he said quietly, ''my identity explains nothing, least of all the abysmal way I treated you. Obviously seeing you again has come as a shock to me. I don't know your aunt, or anything about her contract.''

''Well, whatever,'' she said, trying to shrug carelessly, knowing she could not allow that sincere tone to disarm her.

''Jordan, why are you in Penwyck?'' he asked.

How dearly she would have loved to tell him she was here for a meeting of municipalities. That she was the best mayor in the world and she had come to receive a medal.

Childish to want to build herself up like that, just because he was a prince and she was a kitchen assistant. ''I'm working with my aunt on the banquet preparations for next Saturday. Whitney, we have to leave.'' This room, this castle, this island.

Whitney gave her an amazed look. "I not leaving. You leave."

Not now, she begged inwardly. This would be the worst possible timing for that stubborn streak to put in an appearance. "Whitney," Jordan said, using her sternest mother voice, "we are leaving right now." She held out her hand.

Whitney ignored it, studying the chess players with single-minded intensity.

"Don't you dare laugh," Jordan warned Ben. Owen. The prince. His Royal Highness. She had to get out of here.

"I'm not laughing," he denied. "Whitney, please do as your mother asks."

"I'm Princess Whitney," the tyke decided.

"All right by me," Owen said easily. "Princess Whitney, I think you should go with your mother."

Jordan wondered uneasily if her daughter really was a princess since her father really appeared to be a prince.

She didn't like how his gaze lingered on the child, and then a frown creased his forehead.

"Whitney—" she said.

A sudden light came on in his eyes, and with breathtaking swiftness he had crossed the distance between himself and Jordan. His fingers bit into her elbow and he looked straight into her eyes.

"My God, is she mine?" His tone was quiet, intense, loaded with that same princely authority that had made the young nanny quake.

Jordan felt both frightened and furious. "If you were that interested, you should have taken a miss on the melodrama with your middle-of-the-night departure all those years ago."

How could it be, after all he had done to her, and all

he had put her through, his hand on her elbow made lightning bolts go off inside of her, made her nearly dizzy with wanting him.

She would not be the same weak, romantic ninny she had been before. She had an example to set!

He dropped her elbow. "We need to talk."

"You know what? Maybe I don't think so. And unlike that poor frightened girl who bowed out of here pulling on her forelock, I don't have to do what you order."

"Jordan, it wasn't an order." But at close quarters like this, she could see the changes in him. He was not the boy he had been. He carried himself with that I-own-the-earth quality of a man, one who expected to be obeyed, who commanded people with the ease of one who accepted it as his God-given right. But she also detected the loneliness of a man with that kind of power. There was an aloofness in his eyes that hadn't been there before.

"Whitney, we need to leave." They needed to leave before she asked herself about that aloofness, before she *cared* about it.

Her daughter sent her a mutinous look, but thankfully got down off the chair and took a few reluctant steps toward her mother. Then, giggling she took off and ran the other way, through an open door.

She closed her eyes, and then took a deep breath. Deliberately not looking at the man who would be king, Jordan followed her daughter.

She stopped in the doorway.

It was his bedroom. It couldn't have been more different than the monklike cell of the basement bedroom they had shared all those years ago.

The bed was huge, the four wooden posters reaching

nearly to the ceiling. All the furniture was dark, heavy, forbiddingly masculine.

It might have been intimidating, except for one thing.

His scent hung in the air, sweetly intoxicating, richly male.

Jordan spotted the little black heel of one of Whitney's shoes protruding from under the bed. She went and grabbed it, but with surprising strength Whitney yanked it away from her and disappeared deeper underneath.

Jordan was humiliated. She was in a skirt, and not even an attractive one at that. She couldn't very well get down on her hands and knees and pull her daughter out from there.

"I'll get her," Owen said with infuriating confidence.

Jordan folded her arms over her chest, tapped her foot, bowed slightly. "Be my guest."

Owen went and sat by the bed. "Princess Whitney?"

"Yes, Pwince Owen?" she answered with amazing sweetness.

"I was wondering if you might do me the honor of having tea with me tomorrow?"

"Tea?" Whitney responded uncertainly. "I'm not old enough to dwink tea."

"In Penwyck we call it having tea but it's really like, um, snack time. You don't have to have tea, though you might like the strawberry flavor with cream."

"Stwawbewwy with cweam," Whitney contemplated from under the bed.

"And, there are always treats. Scones are my favorites."

"I don't like those," Whitney decided, though Jordan knew for a fact her daughter wouldn't know what a scone was if it bit her on the nose.

"Sometimes the palace chef—we call her Cookie—makes cupcakes shaped like clowns when we have small guests for tea."

"Does she put flowews in her cupcakes?" Whitney asked.

"Flour? I think so."

"No, flowers," Jordan told him testily.

"Who would put flowers in their cupcakes?" he asked, incredulous.

"The caterer of your big returned-home-safely celebration."

"Oh." He looked dark. "I didn't really want a celebration. My father's ill and my brother's away, and it just seems like the timing is off. On the other hand, is that what brought you here?"

She nodded.

"Ah, something to celebrate after all." He bent over and lifted the bed skirt. "Princess Whitney?"

"Yes, Pwince Owen?" This said ever-so-sweetly.

"If you come out from under the bed you and your mother can have tea with me tomorrow in the garden with clown cupcakes."

Silence.

"I understand there might be a pony there, as well."

Jordan's charming daughter shot out from under the bed, and into the prince's arms. She kissed him messily on the cheek, and danced over to her mother, caught her hand.

"See you tommowow, Pwince Owen."

Jordan refused to look into his face, not sure she could have prevented herself from smacking him if a smug, superior look was there. There were probably penalties for smacking a prince. There was probably a dungeon here!

So, she took her daughter's proffered hand and marched from the room with her dignity barely intact. He might very well be lord and master of everything on this island, but he could not force her to have tea with him!

Chapter Three

"With all due respect, Your Royal Highness, you don't seem to be with us today."

Owen, who had been trying to decide if he liked Jordan's hair bobbed just below her ears, the way it was now, or long, the way it had been back then, came back to the here and now abruptly.

They were in the Royal Elite Team's briefing office. It had the look of a military staging area, walls covered in maps and bulletins and photos. Men, some in uniforms, some in white shirts rolled up at the cuffs, all armed, were gathered around an oval table, taking notes, asking questions, consulting files.

These people, to a man—Gage Weston, Cole Everson, Harrison Monteque—had that way about them that inspired confidence. They were men who radiated strength, and calm, a certain steely resolve. They carried themselves with the innate confidence and grace of men whose strength had been tried, and tested, whose strength had won.

Owen looked at Admiral Monteque who had addressed him. "My apologies, Harrison. Really, I can't remember anything else. We've gone over this a dozen times. I only saw the one man's face, and that unusual tattoo on his forearm. I've described it as much as I can."

"And due to that description we've confirmed who at least one of the major players is," the Admiral said. "Gunther Westbury."

Yesterday, Owen thought, he would have cared, and might have tried to pry more information out of these men, though if they had decided not to tell him, no amount of pulling rank would ever persuade them otherwise.

"Tell us once more, please, about the reference to diamonds."

Owen found he had more important things on his mind. A tea party. Clown cupcakes. A suitable pony. Blond hair.

"I only spoke to Westbury for moments." He stole a look at his watch. "As I've said, he seemed to think he had plenty of time to interrogate me later, and that I was going to tell him about diamonds. I wonder if he's like the children of Penwyck, who grow up believing there might be diamonds in the old abandoned coal mines near their homes."

The Admiral got up from his chair, came over and clapped Owen on the shoulder, a gesture of familiarity that few people would have had the confidence to pull off.

But one of the things Owen admired about the Admiral and all of these men, was that they were respectful, but never subservient. In their company, he felt he was with equals.

The admiral said, "Your memory is remarkable, Prince Owen. I guess that's why I keep prying, hoping there might be one more detail in there that would help us find these criminals. I want you to know if you were ever in court, I'd want you on my side as a witness."

"And," Gage added, "if we're ever in a fight, I'd want you on my side. Busted the bastard's nose. Good for you, though rather a wasted skill in a bloody monarch, no disrespect intended."

"None taken," Owen said. "In fact, if my life wasn't already mapped out for me, I think I'd rather enjoy being a part of the Royal Elite Team."

Gage regarded him thoughtfully. "If you ever find yourself in need of a job, come see me first."

The other men laughed at that, because it was ludicrous, of course, that a crown prince would ever need employment, but Owen registered the message underlying the seemingly light statement. The older man respected him, and given Gage's history, his reputation for toughness and professionalism, he appreciated it.

"So are you heading up into the hills today, sir?" Everson asked.

Since his return to Penwyck, Owen had been trying to soothe his restless spirit, to come to terms with the discoveries he had made while imprisoned, by exploring the rugged forests of the Penleigh Hills and the jagged peaks of the Aronleigh Mountains. Because the kidnappers had not yet been brought to justice, it was necessary to have security teams with him. He took a certain delight in outdistancing them—in going higher and faster than others could go.

"No, I'm staying here. I'll be at the palace all day."

"My men will be relieved to hear that. You've been

wearing them out by the dozen since you returned,'' Everson said with a grin.

"Sorry."

"Are you kidding? They're all becoming quite fit, not to mention qualified in mountain and deep-woods training at no cost to the government."

Owen thought, again, how comfortable he was in these kinds of rooms with these kinds of men.

Had he been born differently, he wondered if he would have been drawn to this line of work, to jobs that offered danger and excitement, that challenged physical and mental strength, that made a man become his best. But maybe that lifestyle was no more conducive to "normal" than the one he had now.

Normal had an almost seductive appeal since his time spent in captivity.

"About that other matter," the Admiral said, and passed him a slip of paper, "here's that information you requested."

Owen unfolded the paper. Whitney Mary Ashbury. Born in Wintergreen, Connecticut, St. Paul's Hospital, April 15, four years ago. Nine months from those July days when he had frolicked with Jordan.

He had a daughter. A beautiful little girl, with her mother's blond hair, and his own blue eyes. And if he was a normal man, he would not have missed a second of the miracle of fatherhood. He would have seen Jordan grow round with his child, held her hand during the moment their love burst into the world in such an incredible form.

If he was a normal man, there would have been a little house that they would have picked furniture for together. They would have had a puppy and a barbecue in a backyard surrounded by a white picket fence. He would have had to put the swing set together himself. They would have had a dog that chased a Frisbee and slept under the baby's carriage when she was out in the yard.

He imagined that being normal—coming home to Jordan.

The thought was so appealing it caused him pain.

He had experienced what it was like to be normal for those few weeks in America. What it was not to be in the spotlight. What it was to hold hands with a girl, and even kiss her publicly, and no flashbulbs went off, no microphones were shoved in his face.

He had known then that a man could make himself insane wishing to be things he was not, wishing to have things he knew he could not have.

But now she was here. He had been given a second chance. He had lain awake last night, thinking how remarkable it was that he had reached the conclusion that giving up Jordan had been the worst mistake of his life, and then by some astonishing coincidence here she was, right on Penwyck, right in the castle.

Of course, as the night had progressed, he had realized it was no coincidence. He had probably been naive to think he was on his own that summer.

Some of these men in this very room might have tailed him through his first love. Watched dispassionately as he had stolen his first kiss, grown bolder, made love to her on a beach that he was sure had been empty. He wondered, now, how he could have been so naive as to think they had just let him go. But he felt angry, too. Invaded. The tender secret he had nurtured inside himself probably documented in a thick dossier somewhere.

Had any of them known about his daughter? Who had they reported to?

It came to him with crystal clarity. His mother.

"Gentlemen," he said, suddenly not enjoying their company at all anymore, "I hope you'll excuse me. I have an appointment."

"Can we schedule another meeting?" the admiral asked.

"If we have to," Owen agreed, resignedly, and left after setting a future date and promising to call if he remembered anything new, no matter how minute.

His next stop was the kitchen—not the banquet kitchen that was just opened and staffed for special occasions but the regular palace kitchen.

Cookie was in a sour mood, and she glowered at Owen when he came in. Like many cooks, she had a weakness for her own wares, which she packed around on a huge frame.

"They should have asked me to supervise your celebration," she told him, waving a spoon at him, her curly, gray hair echoing her indignation by springing wildly out from under her hat. "I'm the one that knows all your favorites. That woman down there in the banquet kitchen is a disgrace. I went and had me a look at her operation and you've never seen such goings-on. I think she's using bat wings and eye of newt in those concoctions. If you value your life, don't eat anything on Saturday night. Not one thing!"

Owen regarded Cookie fondly. She was ancient and had been offered retirement many times. She refused with great hauteur, and ignored the young chefs who were hired to lighten her load. Asking her to cook for a huge crowd at her age would be unthinkable, and she knew it, but loved to protest, anyway.

"Ah, Cookie, the queen is trying to prevent word from getting out that my favorite food is hot dogs roasted to nearly black."

She looked slightly mollified by that, so Owen continued, "I've come to ask a favor, something that's far more important to me than the celebration on Saturday night."

The sour expression receded slightly from her face.

"I've invited an old acquaintance and her young daughter for afternoon tea in the back garden." Not a good time to mention Jordan was with the enemy camp. "Do you think you could do something that puts her in a frame of mind to, er, really enjoy herself?"

Cookie's eyes nearly disappeared in the wrinkles caused by her smile. "Count on me, Your Royal Highness. I know just the thing."

"I might have mentioned the clown cupcakes to the child," Owen hinted.

"You did, did you? You haven't had those since you were nine years old."

"They made a lasting impression."

Cookie's smile deepened. "Clown cupcakes it is. And you leave the rest to me. She'll enjoy herself. A little aphrodisiac in the tea, perhaps?"

"Cookie!" he said, not letting on exactly how appealing it would be if he could use a potion to overcome Jordan's prickliness, instead of his own charm, which she had seemed immune to yesterday.

The old cook cackled with fiendish delight, and shooed him out of her kitchen. "The back garden at two, Prince Owen."

His next stop was his sister, Anastasia's quarters.

"A tiara? Good grief, Owen, what for?"

"A very small one. For a little girl I'm having tea with this afternoon. She wants to be a princess."

"Oh, I've seen her! Rambunctious little thing, skipping all over the palace, running her nanny ragged. She belongs to that odd catering crew who are doing your banquet, right?''

He tried not to wince at his daughter being described like a member of a gypsy tribe.

''I've loved hearing her laughter,'' Anastasia said. ''This stuffy old place is ready for children, don't you think?''

''I do think that.''

This earned him a thoughtful look. ''You say that as if you've actually given it a thought, which I find amazing. Owen, is there something you want to tell me about?''

''I was just thinking of Megan and Jean-Paul,'' he said, naming his sister and her new husband, though the truth was he had not been thinking of them at all. ''I was thinking how there will be children here again soon.'' *But even sooner than Megan's due date, if things went according to his plan.*

He realized then, that he wanted to do more than clear the air between himself and Jordan. He wanted to win her over. He wanted the love to reblossom between them. He wanted her to stay. He wanted his child raised here.

But the look on Jordan's face yesterday when she had marched out of his quarters really didn't bode well for what he wanted at all. The only time the look on her face had softened was when her eyes came to rest on her daughter.

Maybe if he could win Whitney first…

''A tiara it is. I'll be back in a minute.'' His sister disappeared into her bedroom and came back out momentarily. ''Here take this. It's so lovely and it's the smallest one I have.''

He looked at the tiara his sister held out to him. It

was tiny and beautiful, studded with what looked to be real diamonds.

"Is it valuable?" he asked, suddenly uncertain about what was an appropriate gift for a young girl. Then he reminded himself, it wasn't any little girl. It was his daughter.

"Well, you don't want her to flush it down the loo," his sister smiled, "but really it only has value if it brings joy."

Next, Owen visited the stables. He was happy to find a fat pony named Tubby was alive and well. Tubby stood only three and a half feet high at the wither. He was nearly as wide as he was high. He had a deep gold coat and a long blond mane that very nearly swept the ground, and a tail that did sweep the ground. Owen took great pleasure in brushing the pony himself, selecting the tack for it, putting on the bridle and saddle.

He had missed so much. Whitney's birth, choosing a name for her, her first words and her first steps. But he got to give his daughter her first pony ride.

As he became more engrossed in his arrangements for the tea party, Owen was not sure he could remember ever feeling anything like the deep delight that was swelling in him as he planned, as he imagined the look on Whitney's face, and the look on her mother's as she saw him demonstrating his caring for his daughter.

It occurred to him that he was happy.

And that he had not been truly happy since he had been escorted home from California five years ago. He had been busy. And productive. He had smiled in all the right places. He had cared about all the right causes. He had done exactly as he was expected to do.

And it had not brought him one moment of feeling

like this: quietly glowing, his heart breaking out of the ice that had formed around it.

He went to the back garden next. A wrought iron table and chairs were being set out in the old cobblestone courtyard. He chose a plaid tablecloth and matching pads for the chairs, an arrangement of fall squash in a basket as a centerpiece.

He noticed a young gardener working enthusiastically, and went over and introduced himself as he always did when he came across staff at the castle he did not know.

"Most of the flowers are done for the year, Your Royal Highness," Ralph explained, shy at Owen's personal interest. "We had a dreadful early frost. But I've brought some buckets of chrysanthemums for fall color, and I've been robbing marigolds from all over the grounds and replanting them here. Also, I swiped the fall blooming crocuses from the front beds. I seem to be competing with some nut in the banquet kitchen, but I told her I had priority. I do, don't I, sir?"

"You certainly do have priority," Owen said, amused despite the fact the nut might very well be Jordan.

"If you want, I'll bring some fall leaves, and make a pile over there for the little girl to play in. And I could weave some maple branches over the arbor, so they could enter the garden through a tunnel of red and yellow."

"How did you know about the little girl?" Owen asked, surprised.

"Her nanny, Trisha, is my friend as well as Cookie's granddaughter, and so she heard about the cupcakes."

"So, is the castle abuzz?"

"No, sir. Of course not. When I told Trisha I'd been assigned to work here today, she told me why. That you had special guests. That's all."

The guilty way he said, *that's all*, made Owen realize it probably wasn't.

"Thank you for making it so special," Owen said. "I appreciate it."

The boy blushed and looked at his toe, obviously debating, then blurted out in a rush, "Trisha, told me your, er, lady friend, isn't very happy about all this."

"She isn't?"

The boy was looking uncomfortable. "Frothing mad is what Trisha said."

"What else did Trisha say?"

"Well, ah, the lady might try to get out of staying for tea. Might beg off that she's needed in the kitchen."

"So why are you going to all this trouble?"

"I guess I thought if I made it really pretty, she wouldn't be able to resist staying. Kind of like a fairy tale."

Owen smiled. "Why would you do that for me?"

"Loyalty, sir. But I kind of have this feeling for Trisha, and I tried to think what she would like, what might make her see me differently." The boy suddenly looked around, obviously aghast at how personal he had gotten with the prince, discussing the pitfalls of unrequited love.

He glanced around. "I've forgotten me place," he mumbled. "I'll just get back to work now, sir."

"Would the garden look nice in the evening?"

"Oh, yes sir. It would. You could put some small white lights in amongst the flowers and drape those light nets over the shrubs. It would be extraordinary."

"Do that for me, as well, then."

"Yes, Your Royal Highness."

"At 8:00 p.m," Owen said softly, "I'll have Cookie

deliver a carafe of hot chocolate and a plate of those chocolate dipped wafers. Would your girl like that?''

''For me?'' the boy whispered. ''For me and Trisha?''

''No sense having us both strike out after all the work you've done.''

''Thank you, Your Royal Highness,'' Ralph stammered. ''I'll never forget it.''

''Well,'' Owen said with a sigh, looking around the beautiful garden after the boy had departed, ''apparently it has no value unless it brings joy.''

Taking a deep breath, he headed for the banquet kitchen. He realized he had made the assumption that winning Jordan back was going to be easy, that she would be as powerless in the face of their shared passion as he felt he was.

Now he could see it was going to be like playing a very difficult game of chess.

Thankfully, Jordan was not in the kitchen.

''Who's in charge here?'' he asked. And he made his deal.

Jordan arrived late and breathless. Owen sat at the table and watched her and Whitney come hand in hand through the arbor.

He noticed, amused, Jordan still underplayed her every asset. Her hair was in a maintenance-free style, she wore no makeup, she was in a dowdy gray slack suit that disguised any curves she might have. He thought he'd seen prison uniforms that were slightly more appealing than the outfit Jordan had on.

And despite that, pure energy crackled in the air around her, just as it had always done. Her eyes snapped blue heated sparks. His mouth went dry when he remembered what it was to have all that energy and all that heat brought to him, willingly.

Her jaw had a familiar stubborn set to it, and he realized he better not hold his breath waiting for the willingly part of it.

His daughter was in a red beret, and a lovely white sweater, a plaid skirt and red tights.

He watched with pleasure, as they both stopped under the arbor and looked up, bathed in astonishing color as sunlight filtered through the branches Ralph had put there.

"Welcome," Owen said gravely, standing.

"Pwince Owen," Whitney said. Somebody had taught her to curtsey, and he was willing to bet from the look on her mother's face, it hadn't been her. The clumsy little curtsey was interrupted as soon as Whitney's eyes fell on the pony, who was happily munching the pile of leaves Ralph had brought for her. She squealed, prince, protocol and mother all equally disregarded as she broke free and ran over to where Tubby was firmly in the groom's grasp.

Owen was glad Ralph had warned him, because he would have been bitterly disappointed if he expected Jordan to share his pleasure in his introduction of Whitney to the equine world. Jordan watched her daughter for a moment, allowed herself to glance around the garden, and then straightened her shoulders as though she was doing battle with the devil over her soul.

"I'm sorry," she said coolly. "I won't be able to stay. There's far too much work in the kitchen. I've brought Whitney, though, and I can call her nanny if you don't think you can manage her by yourself."

He battled the desire to wipe that chilly expression off

her face with his lips. Equally coolly he said, "Actually I've had a chat with your charming aunt. Meg, isn't it?"

She nodded warily.

"She was quite happy to relieve you of your duties this afternoon."

Jordan blinked hard. "Happy to let me have an afternoon off? You couldn't have met my real Aunt Meg."

"This high? Plumpish? Um, eccentric?"

Jordan squinted at him. He remembered that look. *You haven't really researched that at all. You're making it up.* "You bought her," she guessed. "What did it cost you, Blond Boy?"

He thought that might be a good sign, the almost unconscious use of the endearment.

"She traded you for nasturtiums, Blond Girl."

"Don't call me that." Obviously she had now realized old endearments would move them toward the dangerous ground of sweet memory. "And what do you mean, she traded me for nasturtiums? There are no nasturtiums on Penwyck. There are no nasturtiums in the whole universe as far as I can tell. And how did you know that you were going to need to make a trade? That I wasn't coming to your little party willingly?"

He thought her use of the word willingly was unfortunate in light of the context he had been using it in only moments before. It made him want to skip all this—the anger and the awkwardness—and just get to the part where his lips met hers, and her resistance melted completely.

"Palaces are funny places, Jordan. Your plot not to join me reached me before you had fully formed it."

"Oh for God's sake, Owen, you sound like some medieval despot. I was not plotting. I have responsibilities. And pleasing you is not one of them. You have a staff of a hundred and ten fawning, adoring, loyal servants to do that for you.''

''I don't refer to my staff as servants.''

''Fiefs? Serfs?''

''Make fun of me if you must, but don't make fun of the people who are so loyal to me.''

''Misguided as that may be,'' she murmured edgily. ''You didn't really find nasturtiums, did you?''

''That was her price. Aunt Meg wanted nasturtiums.''

Reluctantly, stiffly, her arms folded in front of her, Jordan took a seat. She watched her daughter gushing over the pony.

''It's not nice to trick little old ladies. You won't be able to find nasturtiums. Not anywhere, not for any price.''

He smiled. ''I already did. Fifty dozen orange and a dozen yellow from the hothouse of a friend of mine in England.''

''I hate you,'' she said in a low voice. ''And you may have bought my presence for an afternoon, but you can't make me like it, and you can't make me like you.''

It occurred to him this wasn't going well, not at all according to his script, not producing any of the enjoyment a well-matched chess game gave him.

''Jordan, all I want is a chance. To tell you what happened. That's all. One chance.''

''All right,'' she said. ''One chance. And that's it, Owen. No more vulgar displays of power and wealth—buying the affection of my aunt and my daughter.''

He supposed that meant now would not be a really good time to present Whitney with the tiara.

Jordan was looking around, but rather than looking enchanted as he and Ralph had hoped, she looked decidedly cynical. "The garden doesn't usually look like this does it?"

"I wanted it to look special," he admitted.

"You wanted to manipulate my impressions of you."

"You know, you are beginning to make me feel angry." The statement astonished him. The last time he'd felt angry he'd been able to smash his captor in the mouth. This was a different kind of opponent altogether.

And yet he felt more helpless than he had when he was in chains.

"Angry?" Jordan laughed without humor. "That's how I've felt for five years. I think it's your turn."

It was absolutely the wrong time for the platter of scones and the clown cupcakes to arrive, but they did anyway. The girl who delivered them, insensitive to the mood at the table, fawned over him terribly, while Jordan looked on, disgusted. He didn't think the fact that his staff liked him should be held against him.

Whitney would not get off the pony to try them and Jordan would not touch the delectable offerings set on the table before them.

He ate the entire plate of scones in an atmosphere of tense silence. The girl raced out with another platter of them, and fawned some more.

When she was gone, he cast around in his mind for a way to repair this. For the first time, he entertained the thought it might be beyond repair.

"I'm sorry," he said. "I'm sorry I caused you so much pain."

There. He had humbled himself before her. It was a task that, as a prince, he had not had to perform often.

He waited for her face to light up with gentle understanding. Instead, she shoved her pert little nose a few centimeters higher in the air, and then regarded him down the length of it.

"You know, Owen, I might find that a whole lot easier to believe if you had sought me out, instead of fate dropping me in your lap. You told me yesterday you knew nothing about me coming here."

"I didn't," he admitted, wishing he could take back yesterday and adjust that statement so it looked like he had brought her here.

"It's been five years since I woke up one morning to find you gone. Did you just figure out now that you're sorry about it?"

It occurred to him that she had matured into the most puzzling creature on the face of the earth—a woman. And not even being a prince was going to help him out of this mess.

"I was always sorry about it, Jordan. It wasn't until I had a few days in a dark cell to review the events of my life that I realized how sorry."

He saw sympathy flash in her eyes, and curiosity. But only briefly, and then she quelled both. He pushed on.

"It seemed, in that cell, I had to look at my own mortality. And I had only one regret, Jordan. That I turned my back on love."

He could tell she was listening. He hoped it was a good sign that she picked up a scone and began nibbling.

"When I was only eighteen, Jordan, it was becoming apparent to me I was probably going to be chosen as king one day. I was able to bargain for a summer of freedom. One summer. I swore two oaths to win that period of freedom. The first was that under no circumstances would I reveal my true identity to anyone. And the second, I gave my oath I would return here, to this island, to my life, to my duties.

"People not born to this lifestyle do not always understand the power of an oath. Giving my oath means swearing my total allegiance, with every fiber of my being, my soul. If I were to break an oath, how could people who must rely on me to guide our country ever trust me? And how could I ever trust myself? I admit, in the beginning, I enjoyed that you didn't know who I was. I enjoyed feeling normal. I enjoyed being loved for who I was, and not for what I was. But as I came to know you, Jordan, I would have told you, if I could have. I would have trusted you with my very life, had that decision been mine to make."

"And those words, Owen, that you said to me, that you whispered against my hair, and into my breast, they meant nothing?"

"They meant everything. I have never said those words to another, Jordan. Nor will I ever."

"And is that your oath?" she said, scornfully.

"Yes," he said quietly. "It is."

"Owen, it's too late. You broke my heart too thoroughly, you abandoned me too completely. I have spent too many agonizing nights remembering the sweetness of our time together. I thought," she looked swiftly away from him, but he was dismayed to see the tears forming in her eyes.

"I thought," she said, her voice trembling, "that you must be dead. I thought the only way you could not come back to what we had, was if you were dead. How could you not even say goodbye? How could you?"

If he'd thought the tears made her vulnerable, he saw he was mistaken. She was very, very angry.

"I wanted to. Jordan, I'd only been granted permission to stay for five weeks, the length of the course. I asked, and was granted permission to stay two weeks after that. When I asked for another extension, I was summoned home. I ignored the summons.

"That last morning, I woke up beside you, and kissed your cheek and ran my fingers through your hair. I got up and got dressed. I was going to go to that little coffee shop and get you the cappuccino you like, and a croissant.

"I had become too predictable in my habits. Several members of the Royal Elite Team were waiting for me. It was their duty to escort me home. And it was my duty to go. To not make their lives, or yours, more difficult by making a scene, by demanding to see you one last time. I had always told you it might end swiftly."

"Yes, that was a great comfort to me," she said. She was regaining her composure now, hiding behind sarcasm. "How could that have made it more difficult for me had you had the courtesy to say goodbye?"

"I thought no one knew about you. I didn't want them to know about you, start investigating you, dissecting your life. I wanted to keep you, the memory of you, all to myself forever. I wanted to have one thing in my life that was private to me. One thing about me that was not public and would never be public.

"Of course, I was being naive. I realize now I was not allowed to go to the United States unescorted. Someone has known about you all along. I don't know if they knew about our daughter or not."

"Our daughter?" she echoed. "I never told you Whitney was your daughter." Now he could see there was fear added to her anger. It reminded him of a wild kitten that he wanted to pet, hissing and spitting, getting ready to defend to the death against his affection.

"I can do math."

"You never asked how old she was yesterday. How

can you do math when you don't even know the equation?''

He said nothing.

"You had it checked, didn't you? Never mind just waiting for me to answer! How much easier to sic a secret service team on us! What else did you find out? That I live in a house that's no bigger than this whole garden?''

"I didn't ask anything else.''

She regarded him suspiciously, then put down the scone with only one little nibble gone from it. "Well, don't. Because my life is none of your business. For what it's worth, I accept your apology, and even your explanation. We were both very young. I'm sure we both did things we regret and that we would like to change. But it doesn't matter. It's over and done with. Don't make the mistake of thinking we are going to pick up where we left off, because we aren't.

"Owen,'' she leaned toward him, and knocked the meaning out of his world. "I'm marrying someone else.''

Chapter Four

Jordan wanted to slap her hands over her mouth like a child who had accidentally blurted out a swear word. She had *lied*. She, who took such pride in her integrity, had looked Owen in the face and informed him she was getting married. She, whose closest male relationship was with a cat!

It was a measure of her desperation.

Because, despite all her resolve, all her righteous indignation, Owen was making her feel things that she did not want to feel. It had started when she had entered the garden underneath that unbelievable canopy of leaves, yellows and reds and golds and oranges dancing in the faint breeze, beckoning her forward, *softening* her.

What woman could resist walking into a dream? And then the garden was so quaint, ivy-covered stone walls surrounding it, cobblestones with thick moss growing between them, artfully placed tubs of mums, flower borders abundant with late bloomers, the table set with exquisite china and a silver service—it was all a romantic fantasy almost too intense to handle.

Owen, probably with a snap of his fingers, had set the stage. He had created an inviting space of warmth and beauty that could make even the most hardened cynic decide that maybe fairy tales weren't so bad.

It frightened Jordan that he could manipulate her feelings so completely without speaking a word.

Then the pony. Wasn't that part of her dream for Whitney? If Jordan was really honest about it wouldn't she rather have bought a little farm than a little house? Of course, it was way out of her price range, but how she would have loved for Whitney to have a dog, and kittens and yes, a pony. What mother didn't want to see her daughter glowing with joy the way Whitney was now with her arms wrapped around that pony's solid little neck?

And now, sitting across the beautifully laid table, and just looking at Owen, the handsome familiar lines of his face, the deep blue of his eyes, the quirk of his mouth, the way that lick of hair fell so endearingly over his eye, she felt that treacherous stirring of desire.

The only thing she had never liked about Owen, way back when, was that awful blond hair. Now, even that was gone, and his hair was glossy, nearly black and beautiful. It made some traitorous part of her long desperately for things she knew were lost.

It didn't help knowing underneath those well-tailored clothes was *her* Ben, his flawless skin stretched taut over muscles that she had brailled with her fingers, imprinted forever on her brain.

Trying to think of something else, she looked squarely in his face. She saw the bruises beginning to fade, the swelling going from his lip, and it made her think of him in captivity, at the mercy of someone with a brutal agenda. It made her ache, made her want to cross the distance between them and touch his swollen lip and bruised cheek with her fingers. Or maybe even her lips.

It felt as if her survival depended on him not knowing that, never suspecting how weak he made her, how flimsy seemed the wall of her resolve.

"That's right," she said brightly. "I'm getting married. He's a—" mouse catcher? "Exterminator. Justin Jason." Her voice faltered at the look on his face.

She was not sure she had ever seen such pain in a human being, and she had certainly never caused anyone else such pain. On purpose. To protect herself.

The blood had drained from his face, his eyes darkened to a color of blue she had never seen before, a white line appeared around the lower edge of his lip. But then, almost so quickly she was not sure she had seen it, the pain was gone, and his face looked as if it had been carved from cold, hard stone.

"Over my dead body," he said quietly.

Had he expressed the sadness, the torment, she had seen so briefly cross his face, she had the awful feeling she would have been lost, like a weak ninny.

But this autocratic response brought her the tool she most needed—her fighting spirit surfaced.

"You have gotten far too used to ordering people's lives," she told him. "You have no authority over me, and you will not tell me how to live my life. You had your chance. But I wasn't good enough to be a bride for a prince, was I? Tell me, what's changed, Owen?"

"I have," he said firmly. "And it's unfair to say you weren't good enough to be my bride. We were eighteen, Jordan. Neither of us were thinking in terms of forever. Not then."

''But now you are?'' she said sweetly.

''Yes.''

''Me, too. And his name is Jason Justin.''

''I thought you said it was Justin Jason.''

''I didn't,'' she said with certainty, though of course she was not certain at all.

''I hope he's not as ridiculous as his name. I can't believe you'd want to go through the rest of your life as Jordan Jason.''

''That's because you're shallow enough to think something so superficial as a name would matter to everyone, just because it matters to you. I bet your bridal candidates all have only the best of names and the best of pedigrees, don't they?''

He said nothing, confirming her ugly suspicion there was, somewhere, an approved list of young women he would be allowed to marry. It was a list she was certain she was not on, and never would be.

''Tell me, is virginity still a prerequisite to marrying someone like you?''

He actually choked on the scone he was eating, and she was glad she had shocked him. He looked so supremely confidant, every inch a prince. It would be easy to allow herself to be intimidated by him, or worse, swept away by him.

''Thanks to you I don't even qualify to be a bride to a prince, so why wouldn't you wish me happily ever after, since you can never provide it?''

''Things are changing in royal families,'' he said stiffly, ''becoming far less rigid and rule-bound.''

''Is that right? You have an older sister, don't you?''

''Three,'' he said warily.

''Well, if the system is changing so much, why are you and your brother the candidates to take over the throne? I understand, from talk in the kitchen, it will almost certainly be you. But why wouldn't it be one of your sisters? The oldest one, perhaps? Why can't she become the reigning monarch?''

Whatever slight advantage she had gained by knocking him off balance, by shocking him was gone, he was looking at her with growing amusement.

Amusement!

"I remember you like this," he said, smiling suddenly. "So smart. You scared all the boys away always playing devil's advocate. Did you know that?''

"Unfortunately, I didn't scare away the boy whom I should have been most afraid of.''

His smile disappeared, and again she registered the pain in his face, and instead of feeling good about it, felt terrible.

She rushed on, searching for safe ground. Far easier to discuss politics, philosophies, than mistakes made, regrets harbored. "As for being a devil's advocate, I find myself on an island that has an archaic political system. A patriarchal monarchy, a system that assumes and entrenches the superiority of men. I'm a devil's advocate for mentioning it? Do you see why we can't have a future?''

"Actually, it only makes me think a future with you would be more interesting.''

He said that as if he was really and truly contemplating a future with her. She could not give in to the feeling that caused within her: weakness. A feeling of wanting to melt toward him, erase the hurts of the past with their lips and their hands.

It was a war for her soul, and she wanted to surrender? One day in and she was going to wave the white flag? She needed to be building her battlements, not crawling over the walls! It was good that she had said she was getting married! Even if it was a lie, it was a necessary one, one that should keep Owen at a distance.

"You and I have no future, Owen," she said, forcing her tone to be uncompromising. "I know that. Why can't you see it?"

The problem was he didn't look like he was going to give up and just wish her a nice life. His face had a stubborn cast to it.

"I find myself asking why you've been brought here to Penwyck. Someone with a great deal of power has a piece of this puzzle that I don't have."

Was he saying he might be given permission to marry her? She would not even allow herself to contemplate it.

"Owen, I am not a chess piece in the royal manipulations. I have no desire to be. The sad truth is that you and I had a passionate summer that we cannot revisit. We barely knew each other then, and we barely know each other now. There is a possibility that it is only the most amazing of coincidences that I wound up here to help cook your stupid dinner.

"You should be relieved to know I've decided to refrain from venting five years of rage at you by putting Ex-Lax in your portion of the Dancing Chocolate Ecstasy.

"On Sunday morning, I am going to pack my bags and I am going to take my daughter and go home and back to my very ordinary life."

He was watching her closely. Much too closely.

"She's my daughter, too," he said quietly.

"Don't you even think of threatening me, Owen."

"I'm not. I'm simply stating a fact."

"Well, it's a good thing for me she's a girl, since that puts her out of the lineup for the throne. Or would her illegitimacy have done that anyway?'' She was saying hurtful things to him, but they seemed to be backfiring on her. Every time he winced as one of her barbs found its way home, she found herself feeling sorry she had said it.

"You aren't listening to me," he said quietly. "You are trying to turn everything into a fight. I seem to remember that, too. You were a formidable debate partner. But I don't want this to be a debate. I want to be Whitney's father."

"Nothing can change the fact that you are Whitney's father."

"I don't mean as a function of biology. I want to be her father. A person of importance in her life."

"Look, Owen, money is obviously not a problem. You will have to do what the other weekend dads do, fly over and visit, buy her a pony, take her to Disneyland once a year."

It occurred to her that meant he would always be part of her life. At least until Whitney was grown-up. She could be strong for four or five more days, but fourteen years?

"Give me until Saturday," he said.

"To what?"

"To change your mind. About the man. And about me."

"No!"

"Jordan, something is wrong here. You talk about getting married without an ounce of excitement, talk about going back to an ordinary life. My experience with love is that nothing is ordinary once it finds you. Everything is extraordinary."

"I'm glad love was so extraordinary for you! My experience with love is that it hurts!"

"Are you telling me you are going to marry a man you don't love?"

Oh, God, that was the problem with lies. They started out so simply, and the next thing you knew they were tangled around you as if you had inadvertently dropped in on a nest of snakes.

"I am not discussing my personal life with you!"

"Give me until Saturday."

"No!"

"If it was possible to change your mind," he said slowly, "that's something you should know."

"Don't you dare wreck my life and then turn around and say it was for my own good."

"I just want your happiness."

"You are no expert on my happiness," she told him.

"And if it isn't possible to change your mind, you have nothing to worry about. You can go back to your ordinary life and live happily ever after. I can live with that. If you give me until Saturday to change your mind. Give me a chance to get to know you all over again."

"You can't change my mind."

"Then we have a deal?" he said smoothly.

Oh, this was insanity. It was like making a deal with the devil. But her pride would not allow him to think she was afraid of the power he had over her, even if she was.

"Deal," she said. It was safe enough. Saturday was only a few days away. She would be in the kitchen most of that time. Besides, now was the time to prove, forever, that she was immune to him. To take back her life, and her power, to leave those summer days of five years ago behind her for eternity.

He was right, though she damned him for it. If she

could not leave that summer love behind, there was no hope for her ever finding happiness.

"Let's begin like this," he said. He got up from his chair and came around to her. She watched him warily. In the last second, she knew what he was going to do. She had time to push back her chair and run.

But she didn't.

She watched him lower his head to hers, helpless. She sat as frozen as if she was carved from ice when his lips, familiar, touched her forehead, trailed to her cheek.

The ice melted, and when his lips sought hers, her body did the ultimate betrayal. She responded. She did not want to. She ordered herself not to.

But when his lips touched hers it was as if the color stripped from the world washed back into it. It was as if winter dissolved into spring. Something within her, in chains, released, and she answered his lips.

Came home to them.

She realized she had been alive only in her dreams, when these lips touched hers.

"Mommy!"

Dazedly, she pulled away. Her daughter was standing at the foot of the table, regarding them wide-eyed.

Owen straightened and smiled.

Whitney stared at her mother. "You smooching with Pwince Owen?"

"Um, sort of, I guess."

Owen raised a wicked eyebrow at her. "Yes or no question," he said.

Whitney pondered this for a moment, and then climbed onto a chair, studied each of the clown cupcakes in turn, and then chose one. She took a big bite.

"Will you be a pwincess, then Mommy?"

Owen chuckled at Jordan's discomfort. "Doesn't Mr. Justin ever kiss your mother?" he asked.

Jordan felt a desire to kill him. It struck her it had always been like this with him—a roller-coaster ride. Exhilarating. Full of twists and turns and plunges and climbs.

"Who?" Whitney asked, puzzled.

Owen looked smug.

"Jay-Jay," she told her daughter, taking a risk.

"Oh, Mommy kisses with him all the time."

It was Jordan's turn to look smug, but she knew she had to change the topic, fast, before Whitney added that she also liked to scratch his tummy and behind his ears!

Too late. Owen looked distinctly suspicious. "Your daughter hardly knows who your fiancé is," he said.

"Don't jump to conclusions. That's why we got a C-minus on our final paper. You jumped to conclusions, based most of that paper on unsubstantiated fact. As it happens, I don't think it's a good idea to expose young children to their parents' romantic interests."

"We got a C-minus on that paper because we were occupied with far more important things." Still he had stopped laughing. "Have there been many? Romantic interests?"

"Dozens," she said, and steeled herself to his eyes on her, searching.

"Remember the time you tried to convince me you knew how to drive the stick shift in that convertible I rented to go down the coast?"

"No," she lied.

"You were always a terrible liar," he said.

"Unlike you, who was remarkably good at it," she reminded him.

His face clouded and again she felt no pleasure in

landing the jab. She was relieved when he turned his attention to Whitney, but only briefly.

The man and the child had instant rapport. When he excused himself, an hour later, he had won over Whitney as his greatest fan. Or had he become Whitney's greatest fan?

Jordan left the garden feeling confused. How could she just leave him, and go back to her life as if nothing had happened? Could she really deprive Whitney of a rich relationship with her real father?

This, she realized, was just as Owen wanted it. He wanted her to start questioning everything. He wanted to weaken her. He was winning already!

Jordan discovered her competitive spirit was alive and well.

She wasn't letting him win.

The stakes were just too high. They were playing for her heart, and she wasn't letting him win that again. She would have to see his relationship with Whitney as completely separate from his relationship with her, or she would end up hopelessly entangled in his web.

She arrived back at the kitchen just in time to supervise the arrival of the nasturtiums and keep one of the helpers from pouring the yogurt culture down the drain.

She found he haunted her thoughts, despite how busy she was. Every time someone came into the kitchen, she braced herself, thinking it might be him, but it never was. She told herself she was thankful for that, but late that night when she finally was free of her duties, she thought for a man who was going to try and win her, he was doing a poor job of it. She had expected to see him again today. Was there the smallest little finger of disappointment that she had not? Had she actually been looking forward to locking horns with him again?

She went into Whitney's room beside hers, and kissed the sleeping child good-night. She opened her room holding her breath.

What was she expecting? The grand gesture. A room full of flowers that she could have scorned. But her room was empty.

Somehow, he had the power to hurt her all over again.

Remember that, she told herself. She was still repeating like a mantra, as she went into the kitchen very early the next morning, *Owen Penwyck has the power to hurt you. Beware.*

The kitchen was full of welcoming chaos, comforting noise and activity around her. And suddenly something that never happened in a kitchen happened.

It went deathly silent.

Jordan knew he was here, and turned from the pot of chocolate she was stirring. She looked her worst, a dribble of chocolate down her front, her oldest whites on because she had known she would be working with chocolate today.

She turned to face him, and was reminded he had the power to hurt. Because he was not there.

"Ms. Jordan Ashbury?"

She saw what had caused the silence in the kitchen. The man standing there was wearing a white wig, and an outfit straight from history: long navy blue jacket, white breeches, high black boots.

"I'm Jordan, yes."

"I have orders. I am to escort you to the carriage."

"Go away." She turned around swiftly, feeling the blood rise in her face, as if Owen had announced publicly to the world one of her most secret thoughts. She loved history.

A collective gasp went up from the kitchen staff who were watching the drama unfold with avid interest.

"You don't seem to understand," the man said quietly, "if I go away, without delivering you, I could be fired. I have a wife at home, a new baby."

"Did he tell you to say that?"

"No, madam."

"Tell him I have to work. Some of us have to work for a living."

"I understood you had been relieved of your duties," the man said.

"Aunt Meg!" That screech could not be her voice. She modulated her tone when her aunt came across the kitchen nervously wiping her hands on her apron. "Have I been relieved of my duties?" she demanded.

"Of course not," Meg assured her, but before she could draw one breath of relief, her aunt added, "just temporarily replaced."

"What!? You need me!"

"The assistant they brought in to help me out trained at Cordon Bleu. Can you believe that?"

"Unfortunately," Jordan said.

"She has a gift with yogurt culture," her aunt said reverently. "And she's always wanted to work with botanicals. Isn't that amazing?"

"Amazing," Jordan said woodenly.

"Have a wonderful day, my dear. I do believe the prince is sweet on you. Now that's exciting." Her aunt began singing, enthusiastically, "Some Day My Prince Will Come," the theme from *Sleeping Beauty*.

"Oh, please," Jordan said, feeling her face turn red hot in front of the assembled staff.

"Say yes to the adventure, Jordan!"

"I'll say yes to the adventure, all right," she said,

whipping off her apron. "Lead on," she said imperiously to the coachman.

"We have time for you to go to your quarters and change," he said tactfully, after they had left the kitchen.

I don't need to change to tell the prince to go to hell. "That's all right," she said sweetly.

"He is a prince," the man hinted helpfully.

"I don't care," she said. "Being a prince has done nothing for him but make him entirely too accustomed to having his way."

"He's not like that, Ms. Ashbury," the footman said frostily. "I think I get my way more often than he gets his, if you want the truth of it."

"Pardon?"

He hesitated, obviously torn between the discomfort of discussing the prince, and the discomfort of not defending him. "He carries the expectations of many people. It is a heavy weight for one so young. I believe it has made him a strong man, but a lonely one."

And then he clammed up, saying not another word to her.

He arrived at a door that led outside and hesitated before opening it. He looked gravely at her hair. She resisted the impulse to pat it down. She did not have to do her hair to give Owen a piece of her mind!

The man gave a little shake of his head, bowed and opened the door.

She stepped out and then froze. At the end of a cobblestone pathway was an enclosed white carriage, shimmering with gold trim, harnessed to a team of four white horses.

Absurdly, she would have loved to race back to her room and change clothes, to somehow be worthy of that carriage. Not, she realized, that she had brought one thing appropriate for a ride in a carriage.

She reminded herself she was not going in the carriage. She was marching down the walk, opening the door, and telling Owen to go hang himself.

Still, she had a sensation of this being a once-in-a-lifetime opportunity that she was going to spoil for herself by being so absurdly stubborn. Hadn't she always dreamed of riding in a carriage, through dark woods? Something tickled at the back of her mind, but when she tried to look at it, the thought was gone.

She realized she was allowing herself to be charmed by Owen. All ready, and the game had hardly begun.

She deliberately remussed her hair and walked down the path to the waiting carriage. The footman leaped in front of her and opened the door.

She hoped she had an I'm-not-the-least-bit-impressed look on her face. She leaned in the door. "Take your carriage and stuff—"

She stopped. She was speaking to air. The interior of the carriage was empty. And beautiful. It was obviously very old and meticulously maintained. She ordered herself not to get in, but surely it wouldn't hurt to see if the velvet-covered seats were as comfortable as they looked.

She stepped in and sat down. The door clicked shut behind her, and she heard the slap of the reins the jingle of the harnesses. She felt a tug and a jerk and then they rolled smoothly forward. Now was the time to tell them to stop, she knew. But she didn't.

The benches inside were burgundy velvet, the roof and walls rich, cream-colored leather. The "windows" had no glass, but she could pull burgundy draperies over them if she desired. There was silver inlay in the door handles.

She leaned out the window to watch the horses. It was the most beautiful morning, a mist clinging to vibrant green hills, dawn splashing dollops of gold and silver on the mist, the wet road unfolding. The steady clop of the horses' hooves, the creak of the carriage, the lovely smells of leather and horses and morning soothed and delighted her.

She relaxed against the cushions and giggled. It was wonderful. It was absolutely wonderful to be a princess. Every now and then they would pass a car or someone on a bicycle and she would lean out the window and wave and enjoy the surprised looks on their faces at her scruffy appearance. One man stopped his car and took out his camera. She waved as he snapped a picture.

The road was beginning to twist through the woods. The light changed. She listened to birds sing. She'd enjoy her carriage ride. It was no crime to enjoy an experience so special. But when she saw Owen her message would be the same. She would tell him, coolly—

The carriage jolted, hard, flinging her back against the seat. She heard a shout, the comforting tattoo of the horses hooves changed to thunder. The carriage was moving way too fast, swaying, rocking, bouncing over rocks.

She had the cynical thought that this could only happen to her, dreams transforming to nightmares.

"Stop the carriage!"

A shout from behind. Bracing herself she managed to lean out the window. They were being chased!

Her heart hammered in her throat. Jordan was not sure she had ever seen such a magnificent sight. A horse as black as night galloped behind the carriage, immense and powerful. But it was the man who controlled him who was arresting, black cape flying out behind him, grace and power in the incredible line of his body.

He was wearing a mask! She ducked back in the carriage, and placed a hand over her wildly beating heart.

There had just been a kidnapping on this island. Had the kidnappers come back? Had they mistaken her for someone of importance?

Her rational mind kicked in. No kidnapper in the twenty-first century would be on a horse! Suddenly, she laughed.

It was part of the adventure. She looked out the window again, at their pursuer, drawing closer. The grace and strength in his body was unmistakable. It was Owen. The outfit should have seemed ridiculous, but somehow that was not the impression it gave. Instead it gave an impression of power unleashed, of breathtaking boldness and daring, of infinite excitement.

And then the thought that had been tickling the back of her mind, came forward. With horror, she realized she had told him this! Told him her most secret fantasy. Trusted him with it!

And he was using it! To get his own way! Putting her fantasy on display for his whole island.

He was pulling right along side the carriage now. He blew her a kiss, and she sniffed and pulled the drape.

"Pull over," he ordered the coachmen and the horses were brought to a halt.

"I want the lady," he told the coachmen. "I will not harm you."

She heard a scramble, and the footman who had come to the kitchen this morning, opened the door and peered in. He was doing a terrible job of playing his role, for instead of appearing frightened, he was grinning from ear to ear, obviously thrilled to have been included in the prince's game.

"Madam, he wants you."

"Tell him no."

The footman's smile crumpled, and it was obvious from the look on his face he wished the prince had found a different companion for the day.

"The lady says no, sir."

"She does, does she?"

She peeked out the curtain to see Owen leap down from his horse and stride toward the carriage. She dropped the curtain, folded her hands over her breast.

Owen came in the carriage and took the bench across from her. His presence in the small area was overwhelming. He smelled of horses and leather and man. A light shone in his eyes, glittering and devil-may-care.

"I like the outfit," he decided. "Kind of Cinderella, preball."

"Yours is ridiculous."

He took off a black leather glove with white teeth. Given how ridiculous the outfit was, it made her tingle when he did that. He looked unbelievably handsome, even the faint bruises on his face lending to that roguish air that seemed to fit him so comfortably.

"This is ridiculous," she told him, but her heart was pounding at the way he sat across from her, laughing at her.

"I'm kidnapping you," he informed her matter-of-factly. "You can come willingly, or I can chase you down and throw you over the front of the horse."

She saw he meant it. "I told you that fantasy in confidence," she whispered indignantly.

"I've kept your confidence."

"The whole island knows it!"

"Why would they assume it was your fantasy and not mine?"

She felt herself blushing.

He held out a hand, imperious, commanding.

"Owen," she said. "Stop this. It's silly."

"Isn't that what you need most, Jordan?" he asked quietly, suddenly serious. "Just to be silly? Just to quit carrying the cares of the whole world on your shoulders? Just for today?"

She hated it that he thought he knew what she needed most. She hated it that he was right. She hated it that she didn't have the strength to tell him to go hang himself after all.

Like a weak ninny, she put her hand in his. It felt like coming home when the warm strength of it closed around hers. He tugged her to her feet, escorted her out the door. He let go of her hand when he stood in front of the horse. He adjusted the stirrup, then swung easily into the saddle. He leaned forward, reached down and closed his hand over her forearm, pulled his foot free from the stirrup. "Up," he said and pulled.

She felt his extraordinary strength as he lifted her behind him. She could feel the warmth of the horse under her seat, but that was far less noticeable than the warmth radiating from Owen.

"You're going to have to tuck in close and hold on tight," he ordered her. When she didn't comply immediately, he reached behind her, hooked his arm around her waist and pulled her in tight to his back. She wrapped her arms hard around the iron band of his stomach of her own accord when without warning the huge horse leapt forward.

She could feel the play of Owen's muscles under her

fingertips, feel his breath, calm and strong, his scent, wild and intoxicating wrapped around her.

He turned the mighty horse and pounded away, off the road and down a forest path.

At first she was terrified of the breakneck speed, but she could feel how relaxed Owen was, and how the huge horse responded to his every cue. Her breasts were flattened against his back and her thighs formed a vee around him. She could feel the heat coming off of his supple, hard body.

Say yes to the adventure, her aunt had said.

Saying yes was so much more exhilarating than saying no.

And so much more dangerous. She could feel passion rising in her, that dragon she thought had been slain in her life.

Instead she found out it had only been sleeping.

She regretted it when he slowed the horse to a walk, even though she could feel the lather of its sweat coming right through her clothing. A decent woman would have backed off on the hold she had on him, but she did not feel decent now.

She felt like some wildness in her had been unleashed.

They entered a glade and he brought the horse to a halt. She could feel tears pricking at her eyes. She was not sure she had ever seen a place so lovely.

A turquoise pool was at center of it, steam rising off it, ferns and wildflowers growing in thick abundance around it, dipping into the water. There was a picnic blanket laid out, and a basket. He helped her down from the horse.

And they stood there looking at each other, that familiar intensity in the air between them.

''Be silly,'' he said to her, touching her cheek with

his gloved hand. "That's what I stole from you. I left you with a baby and more responsibility than you ever should have had to deal with. So, today, play. Come and play with me. As we did once. Please."

She closed her eyes, and tried to fight temptation, tried to remind herself all that was on the line. Her beliefs. Her strength. Her soul. Her life.

"Oh, go hang yourself," she said, but it came out sounding weak and ineffectual, and he smiled just as though she had said yes to his invitation instead of no.

Chapter Five

It was not going well, Owen had to admit.

She sat across from him on the picnic blanket. Despite her godawful getup she looked lovely. But he could not miss the tension in the way she was holding her shoulders.

She was tense and on guard as if she regretted being exhilarated by the horseback ride, by her initial enjoyment of the little fantasy he had arranged for her. Her guard was back up, discouragingly higher than before.

She had only nibbled on the breakfast he had brought in, one or two bites of a croissant, three strawberries, no champagne. She rejected his efforts at conversation, drumming her fingers and looking uneasy.

Finally, he laid back on the blanket, stared up at the sky. "Owen," he mimicked her voice, "tell me everything about you." In his own voice, he said, "Well, Jordan, I was a terrible child."

She snorted, whether at his conversational techniques, or because she was not surprised he had been a terrible child, he wasn't quite sure. He took it as slightly more hopeful than dead silence.

"Once I brought Tubby—that's the pony Whitney rode yesterday—into the palace, persuaded him up the stairs, and put him in my sister Megan's bedroom. He loved it in there. He wrecked her bedspread and was working on the drapes when he was discovered. Pretty much destroyed the carpets, too."

"What happened to you?"

Aha. Intrigued despite herself.

"Oh, I got put to work in the stables cleaning stalls. Some punishment. I loved every minute of it. My brother Dylan felt bad for me, so he'd come help me. Our stable cleaning came to an abrupt end one day when we took two horses, gave security the slip and spent the whole day exploring the forest paths of the island. I think that was the most glorious day of my life. I was so free."

"You seem pretty free to me," she said unsympathetically.

"I'm not free, not in the way Americans understand the word. I think that is probably the thing you would hate most about my lifestyle."

"You don't have to worry about what I would hate or like about your lifestyle."

She was talking to him, but he couldn't tell if he was making headway or not.

"Where is Dylan now? He's your twin, right?"

Owen thought it was probably a somewhat hopeful sign that Jordan was collecting information about him in spite of herself.

"Right, he's my twin, but we're not identical. We don't even really look like brothers amazingly enough." He sighed. "As for his whereabouts, I'm not quite sure.

Nobody is. It's not like him to hurt people—he's breaking my mother's heart.''

''Why is he gone? Did he like freedom that much that he has turned his back on all this?''

''I have to say I enjoyed that day of truancy far more than Dylan did. He was concerned about our mother worrying, and concerned about being punished. No, he's left Penwyck because one of us is going to be chosen to be king.''

''And he doesn't want the job?''

''It's complicated, Jordan. I think he does want the job.''

''Oh,'' she guessed softly, ''but he's not going to get it. You are.''

''Nothing is certain.''

''Well, if the talk in the kitchen is any indication, that is. Everyone thinks you're going to be named king, and maybe in fairly short order with your father being ill.''

Again, he allowed himself to wonder if her tuning into kitchen gossip might indicate a little more interest in him than she wanted him to know.

It occurred to Owen that he and Jordan were actually talking, the words flowing more and more easily between them, the way it had been long ago.

''There are things wrong with a monarchy,'' Owen admitted. ''It's like you said yesterday. Why couldn't one of my sisters be the ruling monarch? Any one of them has the strength, intelligence and integrity required. What kind of system pits brothers against each other, makes one seem better than the other? My father and his twin brother have been lifelong adversaries because of this kind of stupidity.

''The sad thing is, Dylan actually has gifts that would make him a far better king than I would ever be.''

"Such as?"

"Well, he's diplomatic. And he's quiet, which has been mistaken for passive. But he's not passive at all. He's a thinker. He's not impulsive, as I am. He thinks things through all the way. He's stronger than me, but in different ways. Dylan's isn't the showy kind of strength that makes for good photo ops. Sometimes I feel like his strengths have been deliberately underplayed."

"You love him very much."

"He's my best friend. I miss him every day." Somehow, Owen had planned on Jordan opening up to him, not the other way around.

Still, when they had known each other before, Owen had to be so guarded about what he said. Now, he felt he could finally say what he wanted. So, he told her about growing up in the palace and youthful hijinks and things he hoped would make her laugh.

She didn't laugh out loud, though he coaxed the odd smile from her.

When the words petered out a bit, he slid her a sidelong glance. She had laid down on the blanket, too, had her hands folded on her tummy, and was looking up at the sky, finally relaxed.

"I had the cabana stocked with swimwear," he said. "Do you think you'd like to try the water?"

"Oh, no," she said, too swiftly. He saw her gaze wistfully at the water before she looked away.

"You love to swim," he said. "That's part of why I brought you here. I remember you in California. You were like a dolphin, cavorting in the waves."

"I'm surprised you remember."

"I remember everything about that summer," he said with such intensity it took them both by surprise.

"Is the water warm?" she said, changing the subject.

"Like swimming in a bathtub. It's nicest in the winter." Would she be around to try it in the winter? He better not try to think that far ahead.

"Why are you hesitating?" he asked gently.

"Oh, you know. Bathing suits."

He was astounded. "You always looked beautiful in a bathing suit, Jordan."

"Not beautiful enough for you to stay with me," she said, her voice barely more than a whisper. "And I've had a baby. It makes a difference."

He felt sick at the realization how completely his leaving had shattered her. He felt sick that whatever they had once had, she no longer felt she could trust him with her imperfections. Once, she had been so confident she had flaunted them! Especially that sharp tongue of hers. He reached out and touched the side of her cheek, but she pulled away.

"I should have written you," he said softly. "I just thought it would be easier if the cut was clean and swift. Easier for you if you just thought I was a complete jerk and if you were angry at me."

"You succeeded. I think you're a complete jerk, and I'm angry at you," she said.

"It's one of those situations where I would have liked to be more like Dylan," he said, "been able to think things through more clearly."

"Did he know about me?"

"No. I mean he knew something had happened to me, but he didn't know what."

"Were you ashamed of me? Is that why you didn't tell him? You said he was your best friend, after all."

"Ashamed of you? My God, Jordan, no! I was ashamed of myself for not fighting my way back to you, for not saying screw Penwyck and oaths and honor. But

An Important Message from the Editors

Dear Reader,

Because you've chosen to read one of our fine romance novels, we'd like to say "thank you!" And, as a special way to thank you, we've selected two more of the books you love so well, plus an exciting Mystery Gift, to send you absolutely FREE!

Please enjoy them with our compliments...

Pam Powers

P.S. And because we value our customers, we've attached something extra inside...

Peel off seal and Place inside...

How to validate your Editor's
FREE GIFT
"Thank You"

1. Peel off gift seal from front cover. Place it in space provided at right. This automatically entitles you to receive 2 FREE BOOKS and a fabulous mystery gift.

2. Send back this card and you'll get 2 brand-new Silhouette Romance® novels. These books have a cover price of $3.99 each in the U.S. and $4.50 each in Canada, but they are yours to keep absolutely free.

3. There's no catch. You're under no obligation to buy anything. We charge nothing—ZERO—for your first shipment. And you don't have to make any minimum number of purchases—not even one!

4. The fact is, thousands of readers enjoy receiving their books by mail from the Silhouette Reader Service™. They enjoy the convenience of home delivery...they like getting the best new novels at discount prices BEFORE they're available in stores...and they love their *Heart to Heart* subscriber newsletter featuring author news, horoscopes, recipes, book reviews and much more!

5. We hope that after receiving your free books you'll want to remain a subscriber. But the choice is yours— to continue or cancel, any time at all! So why not take us up on our invitation, with no risk of any kind. You'll be glad you did!

6. Don't forget to detach your FREE BOOKMARK. And remember...just for validating your Editor's Free Gift Offer, we'll send you THREE gifts, *ABSOLUTELY FREE!*

GET A
FREE MYSTERY GIFT...

*SURPRISE MYSTERY GIFT
COULD BE YOURS **FREE** AS
A SPECIAL "THANK YOU" FROM
THE EDITORS OF SILHOUETTE*

Visit us online at
www.eHarlequin.com

I was trying to protect you, too. If a whisper of what had happened between us ever got out, you would have been plagued by the press. And they can be cruel beyond words.''

She stood up abruptly. He had the feeling she wanted to believe him and didn't want to at the same time. "How about that swim?" she said. "The bathing suits are where? In that little green tent over there?"

He nodded, and watched her walk away, the proud curve of her back, the easy grace of her stride.

She turned back, almost as if she had known she would catch him watching. "Owen, don't even look at me until I'm in the water."

He had shorts on underneath his slacks and he stripped as soon as she disappeared into the cabana, went and sat on the edge of the pool and dangled his feet in the water.

Of course, he did look when she emerged. He had stocked a small cabana with bathing suits, hoping she would choose a two-piece one, but she hadn't. She tiptoed out in one that was plain and black and far more sexy in its demureness than any of the bikinis could have been. Considering what they had once been to each other, she was endearingly shy, though he wished he knew what to do or say to wipe that remote you-can't-touch-me look off her face.

He did notice changes to her body. Her breasts were larger, her tummy had the slightest swell to it. But he thought the changes made her look fully and gloriously like a woman, not like the near-child she had been when they had first met.

He also noticed her shoulders seemed pulled forward a bit. Did worry do that? Pressure? Or was she just self-conscious? She had always been a serious, intense girl, at first she had been awkward about her body. But once he had been able to coax a lighter side of her to the surface, and had been able to make her see how extraordinarily beautiful she was.

How he wanted to see that side of Jordan again.

And to do that, he realized he might have to take chances. So ignoring her protests, he jumped up from the side of the pool and strolled up to her. He could see she was uncomfortable with him in his bathing trunks, her eyes darting here and there. It pleased him that they always came back to him.

So, she still liked him in that way. She'd never been able to hide that—that hungry light that would burn bright in her eyes when her gaze fell on his arms, his chest. She liked muscles, and he remembered her running her fingertips, her tongue along his biceps, his pecs.

With thoughts like that he had better get them both in the water fairly quickly!

"What are you doing?" she said. "You aren't supposed to be looking at me. Owen, stay over there."

"How could I not look at you?" he said. "You are more beautiful than the sun and the moon and the stars."

"Stop it," she said. "Or I'll call it all off. I'll leave. I'll—"

He reached her. She tried to scramble away, but it was too late. He had her wrist. "One, two, three, jump," he said, and leapt for the water, pulling her in with him.

She came up sputtering, her short blond hair flattened to her head. She looked like a drowned kitten. And hissed and spit like one. She cupped her hand and hit the water, hard. It sprayed up into his face, went up his nose.

He coughed, and closed his eyes against the sting of the mineral water. When he opened them she was racing away from him. She had the strongest crawl he'd ever seen, man or woman, but he knew an invitation to give chase when he saw one.

He lit out after her through the smooth, warm, water. Anytime he got near, she would splash him with her feet. But then she ran out of room and she had to cut back. Even she couldn't swim that fast, and he captured her foot. She tried to kick away but he held fast. He ran his palm over her smooth heel, and desperately she splashed at him. He ignored her, and lowered his lips to the dainty arch of her foot where he knew her to be insanely ticklish.

And then the most incredible thing happened.

The moment he had been waiting for.

She struggled. She screamed. And then she laughed, and the light went back on in his world. She kicked hard, landing a solid thunk right in the center of his chest, and he released her foot and fell backward in the water. When he surfaced, she splashed him hard, before taking off across the pool again.

They swam and played and dove and dunked. She reminded him of an otter, so utterly comfortable in the water, so sleek, so graceful. Occasionally she let him get close enough to touch her, a skim of his hand over silk-wet skin. It seemed to him that one second touching her was more pleasurable than anything else he had ever done.

"Woman, you've exhausted me," he said, and made his way to a natural bench that formed under the water on one side of the pool. He sat on it, leaned his head against the slick bank, felt the turquoise water lapping against his chest.

He looked up through the canopy of trees at the sky. Content with the progress he had made, he closed his eyes.

He heard her coming, and was careful not to move, not to scare her away.

The water stirred beside him. Her shoulder touched his lightly through the liquid warmth of the water.

"Owen, this is the most beautiful place in the world."

"I know. Even in the winter the air stays so humid and warm around the banks that the ferns grow and the flowers bloom." He pressed his shoulder a little harder into hers. She moved away slightly, but didn't break contact.

"Thank you for bringing me here. For today. I won't ever forget it."

He heard the underlying goodbye, the underlying *I won't ever be here in the winter.* He wanted to hold on to her, to keep her forever.

Could she walk away from him? Was she that strong? That much stronger than him? He never wanted her to leave his side again. He wanted them to be together now, forever.

How could he let her go?

And how could he make her stay, if she sincerely didn't want to?

For the first time, he made himself look at the remote possibility that all the king's horses and all the king's men were not going to be able to put this thing together again. \

It occurred to him he needed to know everything about her. To put on the strongest offensive he could, but also in case he had to bow to defeat. He would then need to have little pieces of her soul that he could mull over during the lonely nights when she was not with him.

He took a deep breath. "Tell me everything. Why you aren't mayor of Wintergreen by now, and what it was like when our daughter took her first step and if you ever thought of me.''

He glanced at her out of the corner of his eye. The physical exertion had relaxed her. He wanted to remember her like this: with her short hair curling around her ears, and moisture beading on her face. She looked like a little woodland pixie, beautiful, mysterious, enchanted.

For a long time she was silent. Just when he thought she was not going to say anything, she said, ''I wasn't sure what I wanted when I got home from California. My whole world seemed to be turned on end. Before I met you, I was the smart girl, uptight, master of the cutting remark. I was ambitious and intelligent.

''And then you showed me this whole other side of myself. You weren't threatened by me and because you seemed to love me exactly as I was I became what I had never been before—this girl full of light and love and laughter. When you walked away from that, I just didn't know who I was or what I wanted to be.

''And then I found out I was pregnant.''

''Did you think about an abortion?'' he asked her.

''Of course! But in the end, I simply couldn't. The child was the part of you I got to keep.

''After Whitney was born, my Aunt Meg offered me the job with Botanical Bliss. It seemed like such a god-send because I was so mixed up, felt so much older and wiser in some ways and so much younger and more confused in others. I didn't feel so sure I wanted to take the world by storm, anymore. I didn't feel so sure about anything as I once had.

''You know what? Whitney's made it all worth it. She's worth every sacrifice, and if some dreams were left by the wayside, she replaced them with new ones. Being a good mom is making just as much of a contribution to the world as being a good mayor. Maybe more. She showed me that.

"I work with unwed mothers, too. I run a little support group for them. It's the same tragic story over and over again. My story over and over again. Women who are too young giving away too much to men who use them and discard them all too willingly."

He drew a deep breath. So this was how she had managed to keep the flame of anger alive so long, kept it burning so brightly. She dealt in men betraying women on a regular basis.

"I didn't know you were pregnant, Jordan. Surely that's a difference in the story. It's not as if we didn't take precautions."

"To regret it all would be to regret Whitney."

"Tell me more about Whitney," he said, after she'd been silent too long.

"I hoped her first word would be Mommy, of course," Jordan said, and smiled with soft remembrance, "but it wasn't."

"What was it?"

"It's awful. You don't want to know."

"It can't be that awful. And even if it is, I do want to know."

"Her first word was poop."

"No!" He laughed. "Poop?"

"Um-hmm. An unfortunate incident with her crawling in the backyard and almost touching some. I yelled, 'poop, don't touch,' and apparently my emphasis on that word had a huge impression on her. She began to yell poop and didn't stop for a week. She yelled it in church, in the grocery store, out of her stroller as we walked down the street."

He laughed, tickled that his daughter was such an

original. "And then Mommy was her second word, surely?"

"Oh, no, not my daughter. I think tuna was her second word."

"Tuna?" he said, incredulous.

"Oh, you know how it is with first-time mothers."

He didn't but he didn't want to say that.

"I named everything we touched, everything she pointed at, everything in the cupboards, everything in her world. That was the extent of my conversations for a full year. Chair. Table. Dog. Cat. Rug. Blankie. Tuna."

"I'm sorry I missed it," Owen said, and meant it. And he was sorry he had not been there to make her world wider, to give her reprieve from those one-word conversations, to make her feel grown-up and sexy and beautiful and interesting on those days when she felt anything but.

"Oh," she said, waving her hand around the grove, "compared to all this, you would have found it very boring, I'm sure."

"No. All this pales in comparison to the miracle you are telling me about."

She gave him a quick, hard look and he felt her relax slightly, the pressure against his shoulder increase just a bit.

"Do you like tuna?" she asked him.

"Yes."

"You see I couldn't understand that. I hate it. So it seemed impossible my daughter acted toward tuna the same way most kids act toward ice cream."

"Genetically predisposed to tuna, poor kid. What else does she like?"

"Um, let's see. Raffi. That's a children's singer. Elephants. Her whole room is decorated with elephants.

Her grandmother painted them all over the walls for her. Blue ones and purple ones and green ones and red ones."

Her grandmother. He felt again the ache of loss. Jordan had a whole world he knew nothing about. He wondered if her mother looked like her, had supported her through this. He hoped the opportunity to know Jordan's world as thoroughly as he wanted her to know his was not gone.

"Whitney likes water, and sand and chocolate pudding. She likes painting with her fingers, and eating with them. She likes funny hats and overalls and red shoes." She laughed self-consciously. "I'm boring you."

"No, you aren't. What doesn't she like?"

"Um, let's see. She doesn't like small babies—I think they attract far too much attention and make too much noise. She dislikes classical music. Sitting still in church. Naps. Rain."

"Jay-Jay?"

Jordan glared at him, and he retreated hastily. "When did she walk?"

Again, he noticed that smile of pure love. "One week after she turned one year old. She'd been scooting around holding on to furniture. And all of a sudden she just let go and walked across the room. No faltering, no falling. But the look on her face! She was astonished with herself. In awe of herself. And really, she still seems that way."

"What did you do for her first birthday?" He wanted to keep her talking forever. He loved the look on her face when she talked about Whitney, he loved how her voice flowed, even and rhythmic like a river.

"Oh, I made her a cake and iced it with pudding and she ate it with her hands and got it in her hair and wrecked her dress. And I took three million pictures of it.''

"Can I see them some day?"

"I guess."

She was still uncomfortable contemplating the future with him playing an active part in it, he could see that.

"What about her second birthday?"

"I don't remember." That was said very quickly.

"Yes, you do," he prodded gently.

"Okay. My parents wanted to go to Disneyland for her birthday. I thought it was ridiculous. She would never remember it. She does, though. Especially the Dumbo ride. A real hit."

"Why didn't you want to tell me that?"

"I don't know," she said grouchily.

"Did something happen when you went back to California that was painful for you?"

She gave him a look that told him she resented his perception—and maybe appreciated it just a little, too.

She sighed, and then in a rush said, "I took her to that beach where you and I used to go, and I cried, and it made her sad and it wrecked her birthday. She was touching my cheeks, saying in this desperate little voice, 'mommee, no cwy, mommee no cwy.'"

He felt as if Jordan had placed a knife to his breast, slid it in to cut his heart to ribbons.

He was beginning to understand just how hard it was going to be to repair the hurt he had caused. For the second time, he entertained the smallest of doubts. He wondered if it was even possible to repair a failure this colossal.

He didn't want to say he was sorry again. The word seemed so stupid in the face of such a huge pain.

"If I had known about her, I would have been there."

He could tell by the look on Jordan's face, that somehow he had managed to say exactly the wrong thing.

"Thanks. You couldn't be there for me, but if you had known you had a daughter, you could have been there?"

He was crossing a minefield. A minefield of his own making, mines of hurt and pain and betrayal. He knew, left to his own devices, he would never be able to navigate it safely. It had to be something else that guided him; intuition, heart, soul.

God, maybe.

He turned to her, looked at the barrier in her eyes, sighed, and leaned his forehead against her shoulder. He felt her stiffen, then slowly relax.

He thought of her alone, finding out she was pregnant. He thought of her finding out that the man she knew as Ben Prince had never existed. He thought of her going through fear and uncertainty about her future. He thought about her pain bringing that baby into the world. He thought about her dreams going up in smoke. He thought about her on a beach in California crying.

"Owen?"

He did not lift his head, but he felt her fingertip on his wet cheek.

"Owen, don't," she said. "Please, don't."

It was the moment he admitted what had come to him partially on that cell floor in the villa on Majorca. Prince Owen Michael Penwyck was a failure. In the one area in his life where it really mattered he had failed utterly and completely.

She was lifting his head from her shoulder, holding his face between both her hands, looking at him.

For a dizzy moment he knew she was going to kiss

him, and he leaned toward her. Her lips brushed his, feather soft.

He wanted to wrap his hand in the hair at the back of her head, pull her closer, tempt her lips open with his own.

But he knew something she did not.

That they were surrounded by security people in this quiet grove, watching their every move.

He reeled back from her, and saw the hurt register in her face. "We're not alone," he told her.

"What?"

"Since the kidnapping, security is very tight."

She sank up to her chin in her perfectly modest bathing suit. "There are people watching us right now?"

"Watching out for us might be a better way of saying it."

"Were they watching us all that time in California?"

"I suspect so, yes."

"That night on the beach?"

"Possibly."

"I can't ever live like this, Owen," she said fiercely.

"Maybe that's why I never asked you to."

"People watching you all the time. And all the rest of it. I mean it's lovely, but it's so impossible, like a fairy tale. The carriage, the ponies, the horses, the fake gardens. It's Hollywood. It's not real life. I don't know who you really are."

"Yes, you do," he said. "For a moment just then, you did."

Doubt showed in her face.

And then that moment, too, was spoiled. A man broke from the trees. As soon as he saw it was Cole Everson, Owen bit back his irritation.

If possible, Jordan sank even deeper in the water, only her nose and eyes showing.

Cole dropped down on one knee beside the water. "Your Royal Highness," he said apologetically, "I'm so sorry, but this is urgent. An abandoned coal shaft has collapsed outside of Marlestone. There were children playing in it."

Owen's annoyance evaporated. "Will Broderick go?"

Cole's expression said how effective Broderick's presence would be at the site. "The helicopter's on the way here to get you, sir."

Owen nodded. "See if one of the security people is wearing a suit that will fit me." He could hardly go as the highway man. He took a deep breath, accepting the weight of responsibility. Despite his youth, because he had given of himself so completely in the past five years, the people of Penwyck counted on him. They turned to him to guide them, to comfort them, to lead them, in good times and in bad.

Cole left, and Owen opened his eyes and turned to Jordan. Her eyes were wide on his face.

"You were right. I have misled you," he said quietly. "I wanted you to have fun. I wanted you to feel like a princess. But my life really isn't about having fun. Today was as much a novelty for me, as for you. My life is about duty. I have to go."

Maybe, she was the one who had been realistic from the start. Maybe he should have just wished her well with her ordinary life, and her man.

An exterminator, for God's sake. How could he wish her well with that?

Maybe by putting her needs ahead of his own. But he knew he did not have the luxury of dealing with this now. He turned and pulled himself from the pool. There were people everywhere now. Someone handed him a towel.

"I want to go with you."

He took a towel and held it out to her, folded it around her, as she stepped from the pool.

He thought it was the first positive sign between them. But then he thought of what they might find there. Distraught parents, hurt children, maybe even dead children. The press would be there in droves. His urge was to protect her. "Jordan, it's not a good idea."

"You want me to know who you really are. Let me see you. Let me come. Maybe I'll be able to help. I'm not afraid."

And he could see that she wasn't.

He knew it was foolish to mingle affairs of the state with affairs of the heart. Dylan would probably never do it.

But the loneliness caught him off guard, the ache to have someone beside him, someone who he could turn to.

Owen, he told himself, you're a selfish boor. "You can't come," he said, sternly.

She folded her arms over her chest and the towel. "You don't see me as your equal in any way, do you? You don't see anybody as your equal."

"I'm just trying to protect you."

"I'm a grown woman. I can protect myself, thank you. I don't need any man to decide what's good for me and what isn't."

"Any reporter foolish enough to get near you would probably be impaled on your tongue," he said.

"Does that mean I can come?"

"Yes." She actually smiled at him as if she meant it. Surprisingly the decision felt right. And he wondered why it felt so much more right to take her with him on this official duty than it had to send a carriage to pick her up this morning.

He had no more time to think about it. He could hear the helicopter in the distance.

Chapter Six

"**Y**our Royal Highness, we'll just brief you with the details we have."

Both Jordan and Owen were once again dressed, he in a gray double-breasted suit he had borrowed. Amongst all these well-dressed men, she was decidedly out of place in her old kitchen whites with the chocolate dribble down the front. Still, perhaps it was the outfit that helped make her invisible. She was able to observe without anyone paying the least attention to her.

Jordan had known Owen only as a carefree and somewhat reckless boy. And no matter what he said about duty, she did not understand precisely what that meant to Owen until the exact moment that man—Owen had called him Cole—had come and dropped down onto one knee beside Owen at the pool.

She had watched Owen transform before her eyes, from a young man into a prince. Not a prince in the way she had ever thought of that position: rich, pampered, catered to, out of touch with the real world.

And not a prince as Owen had demonstrated it since she had arrived on Penwyck: a man who could command carriages and conjure ponies and provide scrumptious picnic lunches with the snap of fingers.

No, a prince in a different way.

A prince among men. She had watched his face change, as the news of the mine disaster was relayed to him. His features became grave, somber. She had seen a light flicker to life deep in his eyes and had recognized it as courage, pure and undiluted. She had seen a firmness in the set of his mouth that she had not noticed before. She had watched him draw a deep breath as if he drew strength into the broadness of his chest. He had set his shoulders with resolve, as though he were ready to take on the weight of the world.

What Jordan saw was not just emerging maturity, but something greater, a kind of agelessness. She knew, in that moment, why people wanted Owen to be king.

He had an indefinable quality that the word charisma didn't quite encompass. It was presence, a way of being.

She watched now, keenly observant, as Owen became the center, as men older and more seasoned than he looked toward him, deferred to him, gave him a respect that went far beyond the title of Your Royal Highness that he was addressed with. Somehow he had earned the deference of these men, and Jordan had the startling thought that somehow, in that wondrous summer of laughter and love, she had managed to miss the essence of Owen.

The thought astonished her. And intrigued her.

A helicopter came overhead, and she looked up at it. Yellow and black, it had the royal crest emblazoned on the bottom of it.

In California he had seemed like just another penniless

student. Once they had rented a convertible for a day, explored the twisting coastal highway, and it had seemed so deliciously extravagant.

It hurt to realize even that had been part of the lie, the deception he had played on her. He could have bought that car and ten more like it without blinking an eye.

And yet, looking at his face now, she was so taken with the absolute integrity she saw there. Who was he really? Had she ever known? Did she want to know? What would it cost her to find out?

What would it cost her to walk away without finding out?

Somewhere, she realized it had gone beyond choice. She felt compelled to discover who this man she had once thought she loved so deeply and so completely really was. She didn't just want to go with him, she *had* to go with him.

As the helicopter landed in the little glade Owen broke from the knot of men that surrounded him, and came back to her. He took her elbow and leaned close.

"Have you ever ridden in a helicopter before?" he shouted above the noise.

She shook her head. With all that was going on, and all that he was the center of, he had remembered her, thought of her protectively, even after her stern insistence she did not need his protection. She tried to guard against the warmth that caused in her, but she was not completely successful, anymore than she had been completely successful at guarding her heart from him this day.

It had been a long time since someone had looked after her.

"Keep your head down as you approach and exit it.

Very important. If you forget,'' he made a slicing motion across his throat, and grinned, ''chop-chop.''

For a moment, he was her Owen again, not some intimidating stranger who commanded the respect and liking of a whole nation, the extreme love and loyalty of his staff.

Her Owen. Very dangerous thoughts, especially when coupled with words like love. Still, in that split second smile, she saw something. Owen *wanted* to be all that he had been that long ago summer: carefree, laughter-filled, adventure-loving, reckless. Free.

Destiny had deemed otherwise.

So, he had power and privilege in his world in amounts that other people, including her, only dreamed about. He had high-spirited horses and high-powered helicopters at his disposal. He lived in a palace, surrounded by unbelievable riches and luxuries. He was waited on hand and foot.

But he paid a price, some of his laughter lost, some of his irresistibly reckless spirit tamed.

Jordan noticed Owen was as comfortable getting settled on that helicopter as she was finding a seat on public transport. He put on a headset, and helped her with hers, his fingers brushing the sides of her cheeks, making her tingle with unexpected yearning.

But was there any way these two worlds could ever meet? Their worlds had met once, but he had been pretending to be just a normal everyday guy. To fit into his world, would she have to pretend to be things she was not? Worldly? Sophisticated?

She wondered if the sinking sensation in her stomach was any indication of how successful the melding of their worlds could be. She could feel her stomach heading for her feet as the huge machine lifted straight up. She closed her eyes, held tight to the armrests.

And then her fingers were gently being tugged free of the armrest. Owen's hand closed around hers, and he looked deep into her eyes and smiled, and just like that her stomach calmed. His smile, strong, confidant, made it seem like any distance could be bridged.

"Don't worry," his voice crackled over the headset, reassuring in her ear, "it's perfectly safe."

But nothing about her world felt perfectly safe anymore. Everything felt turned on end, just as it had the last time Owen had been in her life.

"The mine is an old coal mine outside of Marlestone," he told her, and she suspected he was not just sharing the information he had received so far, but distracting her as well. "It's been closed since the sixties, the entrance supposedly sealed.

"The children of Penwyck have this distressing belief that the old coal mines might have diamonds in them. They seem to manage to get inside all the time.

"We get a lot of moisture on Penwyck, and engineers are speculating it may have penetrated the mine from above, slowly rotting the timbers. The kids may have been digging, or chipping at the rocks. It may not have taken much to cause the collapse."

She felt the strangest little twinge that he was taking her into his confidence, that he wanted to tell her about it, that he was treating her as a partner and an equal—and all at the same time as taking her mind off the fact they were several hundred feet off the ground in a contraption that didn't look like it should be able to fly.

"When did it happen?" she asked.

"About ten-thirty this morning."

She looked at her watch. It was now just after noon.

"The kids are on the other side of the cave-in," he said gravely. "We think there are five of them, two girls and three boys, ranging in age from eight to eleven."

"And are they alive?" she whispered.

"The engineers can hear sounds, someone tapping, but there's no way to know, yet, if they are all okay or what kind of shape they are in. At the moment they are very carefully assessing how to move the fallen section of the tunnel without causing more to come down. They're also trying to insert a small microphone throughout the rubble so they can determine what kind of shape the kids are in."

"And what will you do when we get there?"

He hesitated. "Pray to be shown what to do," he said simply.

The answer showed a humility she had never seen in Owen, and her amazement must have shown in her face, because he quickly changed the subject.

"Now, I should read this." He tapped a folder he was holding. "It's a bit of information about the kids and their families. It may help me know what to say when the time comes."

His hand still in hers, frowning slightly as he concentrated, he read.

How familiar was that scowl of fierce concentration. She remembered it from when they had studied late in her small room, she dressed in his shirt, he naked from the waist up, wonderfully self-assured about his body.

She felt a little shiver and recognized it. Desire. She always warned her girls that it was not to be trusted, except to cloud every issue.

She turned to her window and allowed herself to peek out. The view was magnificent, rugged mountains falling into the sea, the deep woods, the pastoral farms and pastures. It was beautiful, an enchanted island.

His. His island. His people. His destiny.

How could an average girl from Wintergreen, Connecticut ever fit into this picture? He acted as though he thought it would be no problem, but had he thought it through? The Owen from the past had been so impulsive, so spontaneous.

She reminded herself she had dropped into his lap. It was not as if he had made a conscious effort to find her, invite her into his life. How long before one, or both of them, woke up to the fact she did not belong here?

In minutes the helicopter passed over the city of Marlestone, went to the hilly country beyond it and began to descend. Out her window she could see the cluster of emergency vehicles, the lines of cars snaking down the road toward the mine. Then she spotted the opening to the mine in the side of a hill. Closed up, as he had said, a hole had now been torn in the rotting, flimsy boards. It looked sinister and unfriendly. Inside would be terribly dark and dank, full of spiders and things that scurried.

Jordan shuddered, and wondered what would make a child go in there. And then she thought of her own daughter. If Whitney found an opening into such a mysterious place, and if she was unsupervised for a moment, and if she believed a treasure was waiting for her, was there any question what she would do?

She'd be inside that tunnel in a flash, of course, curious, fearless.

The helicopter set down in a cordoned off area, surrounded by the flashing red and blue lights of emergency vehicles. There was a huge crowd gathered—emergency workers, families, friends, townspeople, media.

As soon as the helicopter came to rest, Owen got up. He let go of her hand, then hesitated, picked it up and kissed it.

She understood. He was not here for her now. He was here for them.

The door was opened for him, and he stepped out, crouching, an exit he had obviously done a thousand times before. She watched, listened to the whir and click of a hundred or more cameras going off, and realized he had faced that a thousand times before, too.

She suddenly wanted to be anywhere but here, in her horrible stained kitchen whites, a dowdy girl, with rat wet hair, following the prince around. But one of the security men was holding the door for her, and she realized she had no choice.

She needn't have worried. Once Owen disembarked no one noticed any other member of his entourage. He was the focus, and he handled the attention politely, but firmly, making his way through the assembled media, the crowds parting until he was nearly at the entrance of the mine. She just flowed along in the center of the suited men behind him.

There was a huddle of people there, set apart from all the others by the rawness of their pain.

Families of the children trapped in that mine.

Jordan could barely look at the mothers, their pain was so intense, so naked. How on earth could Owen do something in the face of such terror? In the face of such panic? In the face of such sadness?

And yet Owen did not back away from the pain, but went toward it, embraced it. Jordan saw the courage that was at the very core of him, and could not help but be awed by it.

He stopped at the first woman at the edge of that huddle of miserable humanity. Her narrow shoulders were hunched and shaking under a thin, worn jacket. Her eyes were nearly swollen shut from crying. Her husband, in green work clothes, was nearly as distraught as she, and trying so valiantly to be strong, to hold her up.

What would they think of the privileged young prince being here? Jordan would have felt like she was intruding in moments too personal to be shared with anyone.

Owen took both the woman's hands in his, and Jordan watched amazed as the woman looked up into her prince's face. She actually tried to curtsey, but Owen stopped her with a gesture that erased the barriers between them.

Jordan did not know what Owen said to the woman, only that she could almost see his energy transfer to her, something lighten in her face, some faint hope come to life in her eyes. She was hanging on his words, and then she was talking, and he leaned closer to her, and listened to every single word. He listened, patiently, compassionately, until she had said everything she needed to say.

One by one, he gave this indefinable gift to each member of this distraught group. Brothers and sisters, grandmothers and grandfathers, each person who was missing a family member inside that mine, got as much of his undivided attention as they needed.

What Jordan saw was that his being here meant the world to them. It meant everything to them that the man who would be their king cared about their families, grieved with them, was here to lend his support and his strength.

No one looking at the grim cast of his features would ever doubt how much he cared, his utter sincerity.

After consoling the families, Owen turned to the

mouth of the tunnel. Boards had been broken away enlarging the hole the children had slipped through.

A group of exhausted-looking men, covered in dust emerged from the mine opening, and Owen went to them next, shaking hands, clapping shoulders, speaking with each man in turn.

Again, he gave off incredible energy, she could see his presence lifting these men up both emotionally and physically.

Jordan needed to be useful, now. Enough people were standing here staring at Owen, as mesmerized as she was by the power of him, by the energy of his interactions.

Not far away, she saw a pagoda being erected, a tent with a roof but no sides. She had helped Meg cater enough outdoor weddings to know that's where she would be able to help. The tent would mean food and drink for these exhausted workers, for the distraught families.

She unexpectedly caught Owen's eye, gestured slightly. He understood immediately and she saw him nod, detected approval in that nod and was annoyed that it meant something to her.

Another set of hands was welcomed eagerly at the makeshift canteen. Aside from being teased about being a ''Yank'' no one questioned her being there, or asked who she was. She blended seamlessly with the team helping to get food and hot drinks ready.

Jordan spooned coffee into one of the giant percolators, began to boil water for tea or instant coffee in the meantime. When she saw chaos developing around the supply boxes, she used her years of experience in chaotic kitchens to help get people organized into specific teams with specific jobs to do.

With an assembly line of workers making sandwiches,

the coffee done, she grabbed a tray and loaded it with steaming cups and fresh sandwiches. She knew who the people were who would faint from hunger and shiver from cold before they would leave that mine shaft opening.

She moved among the families quietly, offering food and coffee. The tray emptied and she set it down to go in search of blankets. That woman in the worn coat was so cold her teeth were chattering. When Jordan came back and put a blanket over her shoulders, she was rewarded with a pat on the cheek, tired eyes meeting hers with gratitude.

To have offered small comfort was so humbling.

She was distributing the rest of the blankets to other family members who had left home too suddenly and with too little thought for their own comfort when she heard a collective gasp go up.

She looked over to the mine opening, hoping to see a successful rescue team emerging.

Instead, she saw Owen pulling overalls over his suit, shoving a hard hat over his ears, picking up a shovel.

She recognized one of the secret service men from the helicopter flight was close to her, and wondered why he wasn't with his prince.

"Should he be doing that?" she asked the man, a nice-looking fellow, with short-cropped blond hair.

He looked at her, and obviously recognized her as well. He shook his head, resigned, looked back toward Owen. "When the prince has made up his mind to do something, there's not much point in arguing."

"Shouldn't somebody be ordering him not to go down there?" she demanded.

He gave her a look that suggested Americans had such limited understanding of how other nations worked. He explained patiently, "Prince Owen is the second highest ranking man on the island now, and there's speculation that within weeks he'll be the highest. Who's going to give him an order?"

"But aren't you supposed to protect him? Isn't it going to be dangerous down there? Geez, he's only twenty-three years old. And take it from me, he's capable of being really dumb." Was that a note of hysteria creeping into her voice?

The man looked as if she had spoken blasphemy, but let's face it, he hadn't been there five years ago when Owen wanted to bungee jump off a cliff on the California coastline.

Still, she didn't like the way the man was looking at her. She felt like things she didn't want anyone to see, things she had not even admitted to herself, were naked in her face.

His expression gentled. "Look at him," he suggested softly. "Look at the way people are reacting to what he's doing. He's a brave man, and they need bravery right now. God knows, Broderick isn't giving it to them."

She did look. A quietness had come over the crowd. They looked solemn and sad, and yet there was no missing the love and devotion in the faces of those watching their prince.

"It is what he was born to do, miss," the man said. "I can look after some things. I have to trust God to look after the rest."

Owen turned at the mine opening, held up the hand with the shovel in it. He disappeared into darkness to a loud cheer from the crowd.

Owen, she thought indignantly, had just discovered he had a daughter. Why was he putting himself unnecessarily in harm's way? It made her feel furious with him. He wasn't even qualified to go down there. What did he know about collapsing mines? About picks and shovels? He was an expert on picnic lunches, for God's sake!

The fury evaporated as quickly as it had come. The strength of her emotion for him could no longer be denied. And now, Jordan understood finally, completely, what duty meant to him.

It had taken him from her arms in California.

It was sending him down a cold and dark mine shaft.

His duty. This was the destiny he shouldered. Owen's personal life would always come after his public one. His first allegiance was to his people, his subjects, and looking at their faces as they watched him go into that mine, she knew he had not been born to their love, but had earned it, one act of selflessness at a time.

Sighing, she took more coffee to the families. She spoke to the mothers, told them she had a child, too.

She pressed several onlookers into mobile coffee service and went back to the canteen. They were getting soup ready and sandwiches, and she pitched in, feeding exhausted rescue workers, dispensing kind words and encouragement.

She made sure a constant flow of sandwiches, hot soup in mugs, coffee went over to the family members poised at the tunnel opening.

She was aware, as the hours disappeared, of feeling grateful for this opportunity of being out of herself. Her own problems and the confusions of her life seemed to dim as she performed these simple acts of service for others. She was grateful that a twist in the path of her fate had given her the skills to make herself useful.

She got her hands on a cell phone and called the palace, spoke briefly to Whitney, and found out, with riding lessons now in progress, she'd hardly been missed. She didn't know whether she was miffed or slightly relieved to see her daughter was more independent of her than she would have thought.

She talked to her aunt next, and even though she had absolutely no authority to do so, she promised she would try and send a helicopter. Meg wanted to send Dancing Chocolate Ecstasy for the rescue workers.

"Will you be able to make more in time for the banquet?"

"Banquet, *schmanquet*," Meg said. "Obviously people there need my DCE right now. You now how mood-elevating it is. We can have Jell-O for the banquet if we have to."

Smiling that her aunt sincerely believed food—and particularly her food—was the answer in any crisis, Jordan went and talked to the pilot. The helicopter left readily when she put in her request, and she went back to the makeshift kitchen.

As the minutes ticked by into hours, she became aware that she felt like she was holding her breath, waiting for Owen to reemerge from the black mouth of the mine. It was evident he wasn't just putting in an appearance underground. He was staying until they found what they had gone down there for.

She would not allow the panic she felt at the thought of that mine collapsing, with him down there, surface. Nor would she allow the emotion behind such panic to come forward so that she could identify it.

The Dancing Chocolate Ecstasy arrived at about the same time as good news from the tunnel. Rescuers had now made a small hole in the wall of rock that blocked the tunnel. They were able to communicate with the children on the other side, and all were alive. One girl was injured, it was not known how severely. She could speak, and was coherent, which lightened the mood of the gathering immeasurably. Also, with being able to communicate with the children the rescue was now going to progress far more rapidly.

Jordan dispensed the chocolate concoction to the crews, and delivered it personally to the families. Her aunt would have loved seeing how it put smiles on faces. Hope was taking a strong hold, and Dancing Chocolate Ecstasy made a wonderful underscore to that.

As darkness fell, people linked hands and began to sing softly.

Jordan had never heard the folk songs of Penwyck. They told stories of generations of people who had faced hardship and won, of people who were strong and hardy and courageous. She felt Owen in the sung tales of great heroism and courage that littered Penwyck's history.

Candles came out, the singing faded, but the growing crowds quietly prayed and kept vigil. Huge electric lights came on.

She kept the coffee and food flowing, fighting off weariness. And then she heard a cheer swelling from the crowd. Jordan raced from the kitchen and made her way forward.

A stretcher came first, being carried by two men. One of them was Owen, almost unrecognizable for the layer of dark coal dust that lay over his features. Several men rushed forward to take his end of the stretcher.

The little girl on the stretcher was conscious, and medics rushed forward. Owen scanned the crowd and waved over to one of the service men. He gave him an order that sent the man running.

Owen returned to the child's side. He knelt beside the stretcher, kissed her on the cheek, with great and abiding tenderness. The secret service man returned, and unobtrusively passed Owen something. It was a small tiara, and he carefully placed it on her head. The child smiled with pleasure so great it appeared to erase her pain and dry her tears. Then the crowd roared, the night went white with the flash of cameras.

The other children, ragged and dirty, tear-stained and exhausted emerged from the mine in a tight little group.

Owen shook each of their hands, had a few words for each of them, accepted sloppy kisses and wiped tears from cheeks. And then as parents and families swarmed forward, he stepped back, and scanned the crowd.

And with her heart in her throat, she knew, this time, he was looking for her. She smiled, suddenly shy, when his eyes found her. He waved her forward, but she shrank back.

One thing she had never been comfortable with was the limelight. She went back to the kitchen, and put on fresh coffee for the exhausted rescue workers. They came and filled the tables, gulping down soup and sandwiches, polishing off Meg's favorite dessert.

It wasn't until a long time later, when the crowds were dispersed and the rescue workers had moved on to pack up gear, that she felt his presence behind her.

"Hi."

She turned and looked at him. He was so handsome, his hair dirty, a smudge of dirt remaining across his cheek, a large rip in the coverall he was wearing revealing the sinewy strength of his forearm.

"The helicopter has taken Alicia to the hospital. And two other children. They want to observe them for the night. A car's being sent for us."

"It ended happily," she said, not at all sure she

wanted to contemplate happy endings in such close proximity to him.

"Yes, it did."

"An emergency tiara in your pocket. Incredible."

He laughed.

"Why did you go down in there? When you didn't have to?"

"Why did you come to work in the kitchen? When you didn't have to?"

"I had to do something."

"So did I."

"What I did wasn't dangerous."

"Were you worried about me?"

"No!" She dropped her eyes from his. "Maybe a little."

"Thank you for caring about me, even a little."

But looking at him, she knew it was more than that. She took a deep breath and crossed the distance between them. She put her arms around him.

And was astonished when he did not return her embrace. Though he did not back away from it, his arms did not close around her, either.

She stumbled back from him, hurt. Maybe it wasn't proper protocol to hug princes publicly.

He was watching her closely, and she saw a muscle twitch in his jaw.

"Please don't be like the rest of them," he said.

"What do you mean?"

"Anybody can love a prince, Jordan," he said quietly. "But underneath is just a man, like any other. A man who is flawed. Vulnerable. I don't need anyone else who can love me as a prince."

Her jaw dropped open.

"I need," he said, "one woman who knows who I really am, and who can love that."

He was inviting her to love him. The real him.

"The car is here, Your Royal Highness."

"Thank you." He held out his arm to her, and as he did so, a photographer leaped forward and took a picture of them.

He suddenly looked grim and tired.

"Not now," he snapped, but she noticed the photographer just smirked.

He looked at her as he handed her into the car, and he looked sad. "It's no life to wish on anyone, is it?"

He climbed in the car beside her, and almost instantly was asleep. His head fell against her shoulder, and she touched his hair, stroked a cheek now rough with stubble.

A real man, who used all his energy, who could not go on endlessly. Who was flawed and vulnerable.

And as she looked at the sweep of his lashes against his cheek, she felt that familiar and frightening unfurling in her stomach.

Was she woman enough to love the man behind the prince?

The press decided to answer that question before she had even contemplated it fully. The next morning there was a knock on her door, and Owen came into her bedroom.

"I'm sorry to wake you so early. I wanted to be with you when you saw these."

That picture of Owen kissing the little girl and putting the tiara on her head was in full color on the front page of a dozen different international papers.

But many of the papers also carried a second picture: a dreadful picture of a girl in kitchen clothes, with her hair sticking straight up riding in a carriage, smiling and waving goofily. In some pictures of the rescue scene, Jordan had been picked out of the crowd, pulled from the rest of the photo with a circle of light. And they all seemed to have that picture of him putting his arm around her.

One of the headlines read Beauty and the Beast, and she realized exactly who they thought the beauty was, and it wasn't her.

She scanned the papers. "Prince's Mystery Girl," "Prince's Secret Love?" The articles were full of speculation about who she was and what her relationship to the prince was. They universally decried her as dowdy and unsuitable, and some of them used very unkind language.

One of the more trashy papers called her a scritch.

He had perched himself on the end of her bed, and studied the papers, but she could tell he was really studying her, wanting her reaction. What did he think? That she was going to burst into tears like some soap opera heroine?

"I'm sorry," he said. "I know better. I shouldn't have allowed you to be seen in such an unflattering light."

"You tried to protect me," she reminded him. "I wouldn't listen. What else is new? Is this an embarrassment to you? That you were seen with me looking like this?"

"An embarrassment to me? I'm worried these vipers have hurt your feelings!"

She looked at him perched on the end of her bed, worried, and she tossed down the papers. She was tired of fighting it. She didn't care what the papers said about her. She had learned, being an unwed mother in a small, conservative town, that she had a place within herself where her dignity could not be touched. What annoyed her about the papers was the fact that they were asking the very questions she was asking herself.

Was she his mystery woman? Was she his secret love? Where was all this going? Where did she want it to go?

She was so tired of fighting her feelings. She closed her eyes, and tried to sort it out. How was she ever going to know what she truly felt?

And then it came to her, how to know. A method she would have disapproved of for any of her girls in the unwed mothers support group.

"Owen," she said sternly, "shut the door. And then come over here and kiss me, the way you used to do."

Chapter Seven

Owen was not sure he had heard correctly. He stared at her. She looked lovely, white sheets tangled around her, her hair standing straight on end, her cheeks faintly flushed, her pajamas askew.

Pajamas. Nice flannel pajamas, styled like a man's shirt and buttoned up the front. If he was not mistaken those were puppies frolicking across the front. They were not the pajamas of a woman who was enjoying a wild life back in Connecticut.

Nor were they the kind of pajamas worn by the kind of woman who suggested he shut the door, and come kiss her.

Still, he saw the light in her eyes, recognized it, knew exactly what it meant. He went and shut the door, came back and swept the offensive newspapers on the floor. He flung himself on the bed next to her.

It felt like coming home to be lying next to her once more. He reached for her, wholeheartedly planning to ravage her mouth, just the way he used to do.

But as he reached for her, he noticed her eyes were wide and somber, and he realized she had frightened herself with her suggestion.

With superhuman effort he looked away from the plump invitation of her lips, and took her hand instead, ran his thumb over the slender ridges of her knuckles, tried to pull the future out of her palm with his fingertips.

"This room even reminds me of the room in the dorm," he said, "and that one you had in the basement suite."

"Horrible, weren't they?" She leaned over and nuzzled his shoulder where it was nearly touching hers.

Slowly, he warned himself. That was part of the problem before. Everything too fast, too urgent, too much about need instead of desire.

"I didn't think those rooms were horrible," he said. "They taught me something I have never forgotten. The magic is not put in rooms by paint and wallpaper and rugs and furniture and a tasteful collection of paintings. The people who share the space are the ones that can make a plain room with small windows and terrible furniture into heaven."

"Take me to heaven," she murmured, her voice husky. "I've missed it so."

So, he didn't have to worry about the shadowy fiancé in that arena. The relief he felt was enormous. Unfair of him to still regard her as *his,* and yet the heart did not always speak in the language of what was fair and reasonable.

All those years ago when he had first glimpsed heaven, he had never once allowed himself to think in terms of the future, of living a reality of joy-filled days and passion-filled nights forever.

Now he wondered if his future could be like this, waking up beside her, holding hands in bed with her, laughing with her, looking into her eyes until the world around him faded into nothingness.

If he was an ordinary man, he could just say it.

Jordan, marry me. Spend the rest of your life with me.

She kissed his ears. Her tongue slid into one. "Why is it taking you so long to ravage me? Is it because the *Sterling Times* called me frumpy? Or because the *Penwyck News* called me a fashion disaster?"

Despite the fact that his temperature was rising rapidly because of the tongue inserted in his ear, he said, "Careful, or I'll call in on the pajamas."

"These are nice pajamas! Practical. Cute! Are you saying my pajamas are keeping you from the task at hand?"

He realized what he thought the task at hand was, and what she did were totally separate things.

He wanted it totally different than before. He wanted commitment, he wanted forever, he wanted more than a quick tumble, as glorious as that might be.

And if he was to have those things in the future, he could not give into the temptations of the present. He could not promise her forever without clearing it through the proper channels. What if he asked her to marry him, and he was refused permission to marry her?

Plus, there was the little issue of her planning to marry someone else.

She hit him with a pillow, hard. "You are doing a terrible job of wooing me," she said.

He picked one up and hit her back. They didn't stop until they were both weak with laughter.

"Foam pillows," she said with disgust. "Do you remember the one we broke open that night in your room?"

He remembered and apparently her memory of how that play fight had ended was very close to his memory of how it had ended.

"How about that kiss?" she said huskily.

But when she leaned toward him, her mouth parted and her eyes closing, he realized, he had matured. Everything had happened much too quickly last time. He wanted her to know he was no longer a callow boy. He was no longer capable of using her, without giving her something in return. His ring. His name.

He peeled the bedclothes off of her. The rest of her was clothed in flannel, too. He decided flannel on some people was what Victoria's Secret was to others. He lay upside down. "I'll start here," he said, wiggling her little bare toe, "and work my way up."

"That will take three days!" she protested.

"That's the idea," he agreed. Three days. Plenty of time to talk, to communicate, to resolve, to humble himself before the powers that be and beg to be allowed to marry whom he wished.

Meanwhile, he kissed her baby toe. Thoroughly. She gasped and tried to wriggle away. He snagged her ankle in his hand, planted his lips on that arch of her foot that was so ticklish.

She squealed and tried to wriggle away. He wondered if he was going to end up with a black eye and decided it would be worth it.

"Just surrender," he suggested, finding her second toe. He kissed it tenderly.

"I have a prince kissing my feet," she said, dazed.

"Just don't let the tabloids get hold of that one," he suggested. He felt her whole body shiver as he took her third toe in his mouth and gave it a little pull. He had a feeling it was going to be a great day.

Unfortunately, the door swung open, no knock. Since the kidnapping he had been on alert, and he rolled from the bed, came up on his feet ready to take on the enemy.

Whitney stood in the doorway, adorable in one-piece pink pajamas with feet attached. Her blond hair was tousled. She had a stuffed elephant, ragged from much handling, under one arm, and her thumb in her mouth.

She regarded the two of them thoughtfully, tugged her thumb from her mouth. "What you doing, Pwince Owen?"

"Um, I was playing 'this little piggie' with your mommy."

She accepted that and wandered over to the bed. He slipped his hands under her arms and lifted her up, put her between the two of them. Her weight was slight and sweet, and she snuggled into him, trusting, accepting.

"Jay-Jay bites my mommy's toes, too."

He felt his whole body go rigid. If Jay-Jay would have walked in the room at the moment his nose would not have fared any better than Westbury's.

"It's not what you think," Jordan said, laughing.

Laughing. Apparently not understanding at all that her toes belonged to him. That a five year separation mattered not one whit. That even though it was not rational, he was insanely jealous that her toes—

"Mommy doesn't like it. She says you never know where his mouth has been."

This was worse than he thought. Jordan was doubled over with laughter.

"Do you like Jay-Jay?" he managed to ask the child.

Whitney considered. "Not as much as Peaknuckle."

Peaknuckle. Well, did he think Jordan would have been a nun over the past five years? Just because she had spoiled him for all time for all other women, did he think she had been celibate? Did he have a right to expect that? If he didn't, why did he feel so betrayed?

Whitney held out the shapeless stuffed elephant she had. "This is Peaknuckle."

It felt like the light was going back on in his world.

"Jay-Jay made this wip in him," Whitney informed him solemnly, showing him a tear in the worn fabric. "Mommy said he didn't mean to, but I'm still mad."

Me, too. Just tell me where he is, and I'll make a rip in him. Limb from limb. Kissing my true love's toes, wrecking my daughter's toys, I'll—

"Mommy says he's just a baby, he'll be better when he grows up. He won't pee under my bed anymore."

"Are we talking about Justin Jason, Jason Justin?" he asked uncertainly.

Whitney nodded solemnly. "Our cat."

The man in her life was a cat! The one she had said she was going to marry. He met Jordan's eyes.

She was smiling, a little abashed.

And then he knew exactly why she'd said it. To protect herself. From feeling all the same things all over again that had hurt her the first time. Except she probably already was feeling those things.

He stared at her, and the truth stared back at him.

She loved him. Jordan loved him. He was going to be given a second chance. Was his world going to allow him a second chance?

Was he going to be allowed a life that included his daughter? He noticed the aroma coming off Whitney, wonderful, soapy and sleepy. Her pudgy hand had crept into his. Could this be his life?

"Would you be ruined if this cozy little picture made the papers?" Jordan asked, and he could tell she was only partly kidding.

"The palace is secure. Nothing ever gets out of here."
Though since the kidnapping he was not quite as willing
to see things as completely secure as he had once been.
And occasionally a staff member, usually someone new,
did get a story bribed out of them.

"Thank God. How could a person live if they thought
their every move was going to be recorded? Every bad
hair day a topic of public ridicule."

He wondered if that meant she had gone from her
vehement "I could never live like this" of yesterday, to
thinking it was the remotest possibility.

He did not know if he had ever known contentment
such as this: sitting on a big bed in a humble room made
so lovely by the presence of the most beautiful girls in
the world. Contemplating a future...

Whitney said suddenly, "I love Penwyck, Mommy.
Can we stay?"

And there it was, right out in the open.

"I don't know," her mother said, ruffling her daughter's hair, not looking at him.

Much better than an out-and-out no, he decided. He
wished he could get down on one knee right now and
turn that I-don't-know into a yes.

The phone rang and Jordan hesitated, obviously re-
gretting an intrusion into their lovely little morning as
much as he did, but then picked it up.

"A call from America?" she said. "Oh, yes put it
through. Mom? Sorry, you'll have to speak up. I'm
what? On the front page of the *Connecticut Chronicle?*
Me? And I look awful? I don't remember where I got
the sweatshirt. No, I am not throwing it away. It's my
best Chocolate Ecstasy shirt. No, you won't be reading
about that next. It's Meg's most celebrated dessert not a
perverted act."

Jordan studied her fingernails and listened. Owen could hear the excited rise and fall of her mother's voice on the other end of the phone.

She sounded…intimidating.

"The prince?" Jordan glanced at him guiltily. "Mom! You're always the one who told me not to believe everything you saw in the paper. Especially that paper."

So, if he didn't want Jordan's life too upset he had to make his move quickly.

"I wanna talk to Gwandma," Whitney said. Jordan looked like she couldn't unload the phone fast enough.

He hoped Whitney's enthusiasm about talking to her grandmother meant she wasn't nearly the dragon her disembodied voice indicated.

"Hi Gwandma. I have a pony named Tubby. He's pwetty. And Pwince Owen is in bed with Mommy."

Jordan snatched back the phone. "Mom, quit shrieking. She calls her elephant that now. I have to go, bye."

And she crashed down the phone and closed her eyes.

"Mommy, you lied," Whitney said, appalled.

"Yes, you did," Owen said, trying not to sound too cheerful.

He didn't succeed, because Jordan glared at him.

"Are you going to do it all over again?" she asked. "Ruin my life?"

It occurred to him that he was going to marry her. And that if he was going to do that he better start laying the groundwork. And that meant meeting with his own mother before he even gave another thought to Jordan's.

He had a sudden sinking sensation. What if he was unable to obtain permission to marry Jordan?

And then he looked at her, and his small daughter, and knew. If he was not granted permission to marry the woman he loved and had loved since he was eighteen years old, then he would not stay in Penwyck, never become king.

The relief he felt at that confirmed the final lesson he had learned while being held prisoner in Majorca. He had no real desire to be king.

Still, he would try proper channels first.

"I have some things to do," he said regretfully.

"Pwince things?" Whitney asked.

"Yes."

"Liking kissing a pwincess?"

"Yes," he said, leaned forward and kissed her soundly on the cheek, and her mother on the mouth. "Tell grandma that the next time she phones," he said.

He closed the door, and heard the pillow crash against it a millisecond later. He grinned and tried to remember when he had felt so happy in his entire life.

He noticed, an hour later, when he was ushered into his mother's quarters that she looked dignified and beautiful, as always, but there were strain lines at the corners of her eyes and around her mouth.

The kidnapping had taken its toll on her, and he was glad he had said yes to the celebration, because maybe it would bring her some joy.

Plus, indirectly, wasn't that what had brought Jordan and Whitney to him?

He went forward and took his mother's hand, kissed it gently. She dismissed her staff, and they were alone.

He had always loved her apartment with its rich furnishings and lovely, light colors. But today it didn't hold a candle to a small room in the servants' quarters in the basement.

"I'm proud of you, Owen," Queen Marissa said, in that quiet, well-modulated voice. "I've been hearing reports all morning about how you conducted yourself at the mine yesterday. Of course, I would have preferred you didn't find it necessary to go underground.''

''I needed to.''

She sighed and smiled, touched his cheek. ''Just like you needed to try and escape from the kidnappers, needed to fight your way out of there, when a perfectly trained group of men could have rescued you.''

''I'm not Dylan,'' he said, and saw that look on her face that she could never quite hide from him. A deep pleasure, now mingled with pain because his brother was gone. ''I don't always think things all the way through like he does. And you do.''

She scanned his face. ''The bruises are healing well. Are you using the cream I sent?''

Of course, he wasn't using cream on his face. He said, smiling, ''I understand happiness is the greatest of healers.''

They were doing that delicate dance that would slowly move them toward the point he was here to discuss. Dylan was always so good at this sort of thing, enjoyed the preliminaries, but Owen had a more impatient nature.

''I'm glad you're happy, Owen,'' she said, and he detected caution in her tone. ''I heard about the carriage, and the er, highwayman. The palace is abuzz with it today. She must be a very special girl.''

So, she wasn't going to mention it first if she knew Jordan was the mother of his child, of her granddaughter.

Dylan would have toyed with it a while longer before getting to the point, but Owen found he did not have the patience for the verbal preliminaries. ''Isn't that why you brought them here, mother, Jordan and Whitney. To make me happy?''

She regarded him without speaking.

''How long did you know about them?'' he asked her.

She sighed. "Owen, it was naive of you to believe you would be allowed to go to America without protection of any kind."

"I realize that now," he said stiffly.

"It was for your own protection, not as an invasion of your privacy. I hired a top American surveillance team. You never knew they were there."

"And so did you know everything that was happening?" he asked, hating it that the most intense moments of his life had been recorded, reported, defiled.

"I'm sorry, Owen, yes I did."

He detected that she was still sorry about something, that she still knew things he did not, things she thought were going to hurt him.

Did she think he would not be allowed to marry Jordan?

"Did you know about my daughter?"

She hesitated. "I did."

"How could you keep that from me?"

"Owen, being naive at eighteen is forgivable. But not now. There are dangerous undercurrents in the palace, as there always are in royal life. It is my sacred mission to protect this family, and the heir to the throne. Sometimes, to do that, I have to make choices that are not going to be popular. Can you understand that?"

"You kept me from my daughter. You knew about her. You knew about Jordan trying to raise her by herself, struggling, giving up her dreams."

"Owen, I understand your anger. On the other hand, you must see that our enemies were able to come in this very palace and get you right from under the noses of one of the most highly trained security teams in the world. Your daughter was in America, completely unprotected, a weak spot. How much better that no one, including you, knew about her?''

''If you would have told me, I could have brought them here. They would have been safe here.''

''Maybe,'' she conceded. ''But it was not the right time for the people of Penwyck to know you had fathered a child with an American girl.''

''Because it would have reduced my chances of being chosen king,'' he guessed coldly, and watched something flicker in his mother's eyes. He realized, again, uncomfortably, there were yet more secrets. ''And why is the time right now? Obviously, you wouldn't have brought Jordan and her child here if you felt it would still be damaging to the all important royal image.''

He saw her struggling, knew that she was a brilliant strategist who had survived the intrigues of court life, thrived on them, because she had always played her cards close to her chest, known precisely when to lay them on the table.

He knew he did not share that ability with her. Dylan did. He felt weary to the bone from it all, the manipulations, the intrigues, the chess games played with real human lives.

''The time was right to bring them here,'' she said, not elaborating.

''And you have that right to play with my life, to make decisions like that for me?'' It was the closest he had ever come to speaking disrespectfully to his mother.

''I hope you will understand someday, Owen.''

''I've lost four years of my daughter's life. I missed her being born and her first steps and her first words. I left Jordan when she needed me most. I didn't know her need, but you did.''

Again, she said, "I hope you will understand some-day, my son."

"If I were to ask your permission to marry Jordan now?" he asked.

"I would give it," she said, without hesitation.

He tried not to show how stunned he was by this easy victory. It made him suspicious.

"Why?"

"Owen, plots that have been brewing for twenty-five years are coming to fruition. Soon, you will know how much I owe you. I hope to repay my debt to you in your happiness."

"Though you cannot give me back that which was taken, Mother, you owe me nothing," he said, concerned by the torment in her face.

"I owe you everything," she said enigmatically, and then she smiled. "I am anxious to meet my granddaugh-ter. Perhaps she and Ms. Ashbury could join me for lunch today."

"Whitney doesn't know yet, that I'm her father. I need to wait for the right time."

"Trust my discretion," his mother said.

And he realized that he could trust. His mother knew secrets—possibly all the secrets of this family and this palace. And she kept them all until the precise moment they needed to be played.

He had thought he would find it unforgivable that she had stolen the first four years of his daughter's life from him. But looking at her, he understood the weight of responsibility she carried, saw it in the lines of her face, and the sadness in her eyes.

She had paid a price for her secrets.

And he knew he would pay his price, too, to be king.

He would hold life and death, war and peace in his hands.

He realized how totally he did not want this job.

"Owen, you are too young for such worries," his mother said, as if she had read his mind. "Go and enjoy being in love. And for God's sake, get that young woman of yours a gown for the upcoming ball that will show her off and make those fools at the papers see how they missed her beauty entirely."

"A gown?" he said. "Don't they take time to make?"

His mother smiled. "How lucky for you that you have three sisters. Try Anastasia. She's closest in size to your Ms. Ashbury, and her closets are full to overflowing. I'm positive she'll have something suitable."

"Thank you, Mother."

"By the way, Owen, I heard many stories of what your Ms. Ashbury did at the mine yesterday, as well. She possesses a quality of humility that speaks to me of uncommon and quiet strength. You have chosen well."

He blushed at his mother's approval. It wasn't until he walked away, that he realized her approval had struck him as different than normal. Authentic.

He was not sure what that meant, until he realized how often her praise for him had occurred in public. It had embarrassed him at times, how she would single him out for attention, say nothing about Dylan's accomplishments, though Dylan would have so enjoyed the praise.

He frowned, now thinking of that.

Had his mother deliberately underplayed Dylan? He loved her, but she had a gift for being calculating. She didn't do anything by accident. Was there meaning to the fact she had never drawn attention to her other son?

He did not want to ponder palace politics and intrigues at the moment. It gave him a headache.

He went in search of his sister.

"First a tiara, and now a dress?" Anastasia said, letting him in. "What's gotten into you, Owen?"

"Nothing," he mumbled.

She laughed. "The whole palace is talking about you snatching the kitchen help from that carriage yesterday and bringing her to the grotto."

"Don't say kitchen help like that. You don't know anything about Jordan Ashbury."

"Owen, I was just teasing!"

"The dress?" he reminded her mulishly.

"Owen, you're blushing! I would never have thought you could be romantic. That's not what Charlotte Hendron told me. She wept after you'd been with her. She said you were an insensitive boor."

"I was not! It's just that she was a bore. I cannot stand these candidates for royal marriage that have been paraded in front of me."

"It's true, Charlotte never would have been caught dead in an outfit like that one within a ten mile radius of anyone with a camera—if that's what you call boring. Besides, no one has dared parade a woman in front of you for years. You always send them home in tears."

"Anastasia, could I just pick a dress without the lecture? Please?" He tried to remember if he'd really sent anyone home in tears.

"Tell me about the girl?" his sister pleaded. "I can't believe things have moved this fast. I mean Owen, aside from on the polo field, you are not a fast mover."

"Things between us haven't exactly moved fast," he said uncomfortably. "I knew her from before."

"From before? That's impossible. I know everything about you."

"Maybe not everything. I met Jordan the summer I went to California."

His sister looked hard at him. "I always knew you came back from there changed. Is she the reason?"

He said nothing.

"She is, isn't she? She's the reason poor Charlotte never had a chance, and why Suzette and Brenda and all those others were sent home in tears. My God, Owen, you're in love with her."

Her attitude changed instantly. "Does she return the feeling?"

"I hope so, but I've hurt her badly. Maybe even unforgivably."

"Come, then. We will try and find the dress that will soften her heart to you."

She ushered him into her bedroom. It was the second time that day he had been struck by how the richness of surroundings could seem empty, somehow.

"Here," she said, throwing open an immense closet door, "Choose."

"Oh, God." There looked to be a mile of long dresses in front of him. He didn't even want to touch them, they looked so frilly and fragile.

"They don't bite," his sister said. "You can touch them."

Slowly, he began to look through the dresses. He had seen his sister in most of them, and her style was not Jordan's. Anastasia could carry off the very flashy with great class. Many of her dresses were bright colored silks, sequined.

"This one?" his sister said, holding a black number in front of her. She twirled in the narrow space of the closet, and knocked open a large box that had been standing in a corner.

They both stared.

Inside was a gown of creamy ivory silk. It was long and flowing with an overskirt and sleeves of film. It was simple but extraordinarily elegant.

"I've never worn that dress," Anastasia said. "I bought it, but didn't like it when I got it home. Don't tell mother." She wrinkled her nose. "I'll get the spoiled little princess lecture."

"Which you deserve," he said. He touched the dress, and almost had to pull his fingers away. It seemed alive it was so beautiful.

"Cinderella," he said, "get ready for the ball."

"It is a Cinderella kind of dress," Anastasia said with wonder. "It will look so nice with her eyes, her coloring." She looked at her brother. "Owen," she whispered, "are you going to ask her to marry you?"

He looked at his sister, startled. "Yes," he said.

"Have you talked to mother?"

"Yes."

"And what did she say?"

"That I had her blessing."

His sister narrowed her eyes at him. "Why do I get the feeling there is a bit more to this story than you are letting on?"

He put the lid on the box, tucked it under his arm, trying to ignore the look his sister was giving him.

She drew in her breath, suddenly, and her eyes widened. "I should have seen it before."

"What?"

"The child is yours, isn't she? She's the image of you, Owen."

"Anastasia, I am trusting you not to breathe a word of this to anyone."

"Oh, I won't. But for how long? I'm terrible at keeping secrets."

"I am going to propose to Jordan the night of the ball."

"That's so romantic. I'm so excited. And I have a niece! A beautiful niece. You'll live here, right? With my adorable niece? Not that Mother would ever let her go, now that we've found her."

"Yes. I plan to have her here on Penwyck and not miss one more moment of her growing up. I plan to be her father."

Chapter Eight

"And I have a niece! A beautiful niece. You'll live here right? With my adorable niece? Not that Mother would ever let her go, now that we've found her."

"Yes. I plan to have her here on Penwyck and not miss one more moment of her growing up. I plan to be her father."

Jordan stood frozen in the hallway outside of the open door. How happy she had first felt when she heard the familiar tones of Owen's voice drifting down that long hallway. Somehow she had become lost in the labyrinth of palace passageways, and though she could have eventually found her way, being lost would have been the most wonderful excuse to see him. To feel his eyes on her, to look at his lips, to maybe casually touch his arm.

It was weak and warped thinking of the worst sort, but a few seconds ago, she hadn't cared.

Earlier, Meg had called her room in a panic and asked her to find Lady Gwendolyn for her. Since Whitney had already been taken by Trisha to see the pony, Jordan had been at loose ends.

And a few seconds ago it had been fun being lost inside a palace, exploring, asking directions, staring in awe at priceless treasures, giggling under the stern gazes of people in portraits. A few seconds ago, hearing his voice had made her heart beat a quick tattoo of delight. A few seconds ago she had felt like the whole world had been sprinkled with glitter as she had experienced it with her brand new heart. A heart full of hope.

But now! Jordan reeled back from that open door, feeling as if she could not breathe.

Not that Mother would ever let her go, now that we've found her.

She stumbled down a corridor, through an unfamiliar chamber, down some steps, getting more and more lost and disoriented. Finally she found a door to the outside, and recognized she was not far from the little walled garden where Owen had invited them for lunch, that first time.

She went through the archway, and it had been stripped of the branches. The table and chairs were there, but the table covering and chair pads had been put away.

It didn't look like a fairy-tale place at all anymore, but like a very plain garden, getting ready to die before winter.

She sat in one of the cold, hard chairs and gazed at the changes. Owen's specialty, creating make-believe.

Why had she allowed him to overcome her first impression, that all of it was not real, that he was a master at manipulating impressions?

Why had she allowed him to overcome that distrust that lived in her, breathed in her, was her, since the day

he had left her? That attitude had protected her. Kept
her and her daughter safe.

She had become victim to his dancing, blue eyes all
over again! To that charming grin. To the unconscious
flex of sinewy muscle, to that boyish way he had of
blowing his hair out of his eyes. She had let that passion
that rose in her every time she was in the same room
with him cloud her reasoning. She had lost her ability
to see clearly what was going on as he had pulled her
deeper and deeper into his world.

This morning, when his lips had played tantalizing
games with her toes, she had surrendered, finally, totally.
She had allowed herself to believe.

That maybe it was true. That maybe a prince could
really love a plain, frumpy girl, a kitchen assistant from
Wintergreen, Connecticut. Worse, she had allowed herself to believe that she could become whole again, that
she could love again.

Now she saw it all clearly. He had never loved her.
If he had, he would have come back to her on his own
accord way before this. A five year break in his fervor?
No, he and his powerful family had found out about the
child, about her Whitney.

They wanted her child!

Owen had probably been ordered to win her over, to
beat down her resistance. She had seen him perform in
the name of duty. Oh, he could be magnificent.

But she did not want to think of Owen at the coal
mine—of the warmth and comfort he had given, of the
strength and confidence he had radiated. Of course he
knew how to do that. It was all part of his princely act.
Those were the very moments when she had begun that
slow surrender to the pull of him, to the power of him,
to the seductive charisma of him.

Jordan now saw, frantically, she had to take her daughter and get away from this place. She had to be somewhere where she could think clearly, and that had to be someplace that he was not. Home.

Wintergreen. In her own bedroom, in her own life where the only one who licked at her toes was Jay-Jay and that did not make her stupidly blind to reality.

Think, she ordered herself. How was she going to get out of here? She and Whitney had to escape. She wiped angrily at a tear that slid down her cheek. She would not be a weakling! She would not.

A young man came into the garden, young and handsome, dressed in overalls, carrying a hoe. He looked surprised to see her there.

"Sorry, miss, I didn't mean to disturb you." He turned to leave her in privacy and then did a quick second take. "Is everything all right?"

"No," she said, and let her lip quiver. "Do you have a car?"

"Miss?"

"Could I borrow your car? I need to go to town. Emergency supplies for the banquet. I forgot to get an ingredient for the Moose Ta-Ta. The shiitake mushrooms." She said the first thing that came to her head. Shiitake mushrooms were not an ingredient in Moose Ta-Ta, but only two people in the world knew that, and she guessed he was not one of them. "I could be fired."

He looked dubious, which she couldn't blame him for, so she poured on the waterworks. As she had hoped, he had a manly aversion to tears. His car keys were out of his pocket and in her lap in a nanosecond.

"It's the red Mini in the staff lot," he said. "It's a very humble car, miss."

"Humble," she said, beaming at him through tears,

"that's me. Little Miss Humble." Jordan Ashbury, the girl least suited to be besotted with a prince and least suited to have a prince besotted with her. How could she have trusted Owen again? What kind of fool was she?

Oh, the toe thing this morning had been such a nice touch. But then he knew all her weak spots, didn't he? He had played her vulnerabilities, the soft spots he knew she had.

Could someone really take pretense that far?

She felt the smallest niggle of doubt, but reminded herself sternly she did not have time for doubts. She could entertain doubts in the safety of Wintergreen. "Your name?" she asked the boy.

She'd have to leave something on that car at the airport so it could be returned to him.

"Ralph Miller," he said.

Trisha's lad. Oh, may they be happy together on this cursed island where fantasy and reality blended until she had not a hope of discerning which was which.

"I hope you are taking precautions," she said, and despite his baffled look, it made her feel good. Her old self—protector of trod-upon women, least likely to be charmed by a handsome face.

She left the garden hurriedly, went to her room. She could take hardly anything without arousing suspicion. She couldn't take a packed suitcase with her to run into town to pick up mushrooms! In the end, she took only her purse and her and Whitney's travel documents. Clothing could be replaced. Not so her daughter! She went into Whitney's room and grabbed Peaknuckle.

And then, her heart in her throat, hoping she wouldn't see anyone, she dashed for the stables.

Whitney was riding slow circles on Tubby, thrumming her stocky legs against his sides, trying to persuade a little faster movement out of him.

"Whitney, love, I have to go to town. Why don't you come with me?"

"No!" Her daughter frowned, and kicked at the pony more feverishly.

"You can ride Tubby again later." Liar, liar. Would her daughter ever forgive her for this?

"No! He has to twot! Twot, Tubby, twot."

At any other time she might have found the pony's complete obliviousness to her daughter's imperious commands quite funny. But not now! Under the astonished gaze of Trisha and the young groom who was giving Whitney patient instructions, she went and picked her daughter up off the pony.

"We are going to town," she said, sternly. "Just for a few minutes. I need you to come with me."

"I don't want to," Whitney replied, trying to wriggle out of her grasp. "Put me down!"

She could see her window of opportunity closing. Whitney couldn't create a scene. "You want to come with me because," Jordan thought desperately and then said with wild and forced enthusiasm, "I have a surprise for you."

"A surpwise?" Whitney asked, and stopped wriggling.

And it had better be good, better than a pony.

"An elephant," Jordan said, in a moment of inspiration. "There's a real live elephant where we're going."

Whitney became very still, and Jordan was able to set her on the ground.

"Weally, Mommy? An elephant?"

Surely she could find an elephant somewhere in Connecticut, at a zoo. Surely, at some later date she could redeem her integrity in her daughter's eyes, but right now she just had to get them away from here.

Jordan became aware Trisha was listening avidly, staring at her with growing astonishment.

"Why do you have Peaknuckle?" Whitney asked.

Jordan thought fast. It was horrible how quickly a person could become good at fabricating. This is what Owen had done to her. Had her fibbing to her daughter. "I knew Peaknuckle would want to see the elephant, too!"

"An elephant?" Trisha said, disbelieving.

But Whitney beamed at her mother's sensitivity, and her hand nestled into Jordan's. It was about the nicest thing she'd ever felt, the battle won, their leaving Penwyck quietly, with no fuss. She tried to smile casually at Trisha. "We'll just be a little while."

"Be back before lunch," Trisha wailed. "I understand you've been invited to have lunch with the queen."

"I have?"

"I've been instructed to get Whitney ready. I was sent a dress for her."

Jordan went cold. So Whitney was scheduled to have lunch with the queen, and she was not. They were all in on it, planning on how to push her out of her daughter's life, sending her dresses suitable for a princess to replace clothing suitable for a kitchen worker's daughter.

"We'll be back in plenty of time for lunch," she lied.

She found the staff parking lot and the Mini. No car seat. And the steering wheel on the wrong side. And a stick shift!

She belted her daughter into the passenger seat, turned the key, and the little car hummed to life. She put it into gear and stalled. Then stalled again trying to back it up.

She laid her head on the steering wheel and prayed. She glanced up to see Ralph and Trisha standing on the edge of the parking lot, looking worried, consulting with each other. Jordan forced herself to smile, gave them a jaunty wave and started the car again.

Jerkily, she headed down the road, her daughter clutching Peaknuckle on the seat beside her.

"Do you know how to dwive this caw, Mommy?"

"Oh, sure. Nothing to it."

Her daughter clutched her elephant a little tighter, and looked doubtful.

After a few wrong turns, she finally found the road to the airport. *Almost there. Almost safe. Almost home.*

Trying not to look as unglued as she felt, she parked the car, grabbed Whitney and raced into the building. She went up to the ticket counter. What to do now? Getting out of Penwyck, out of the reach of these people's frightening power was the first priority. They'd go wherever the next flight was going and worry about how to get to America from there.

Was the girl behind the counter looking for her luggage? Never mind. There was no rule that said you had to have luggage to get on a plane to Wales. "Two," Jordan said, casually, as if she was buying tickets to the movie, "for Wales."

"I don't see an elephant," Whitney said crossly.

"That's because we have to take the airplane to see the elephant." The girl behind the counter was trying not to look at her as if she was deranged.

"Excuse me, Ms. Ashbury?"

She whirled, and recognized the blond hair and wholesome features of the security man she had spoken to at the mine. She'd been worried it was going to collapse on top of the man who was conniving to take her daughter!

"I'm Peter Webster, palace security. Do you think you could come with me? Please?"

So polite. She wasn't fooled. "No, I'm not coming with you. I'm getting on this plane." She turned her back on him. "I need two tickets to—"

She saw the girl behind the counter looking confused, until Mr. Webster flashed a badge at her.

Then the girl, traitor, said quietly, "I'm sorry, miss," and closed her wicket.

"Where's the elephant?" Whitney wailed angrily.

Webster looked distressed. "Miss, I'm very sorry, but you can't leave the island."

"Says who?" she said, tossing her hair.

"Royal orders, miss."

"Well, I am not a fief or serf or whatever you call people who belong to the palace." She drew herself to her full height. "I am a citizen of the United States of America and I cannot be forced to stay here against my will. If you try to make me, I am going to sue you, and Prince Owen, and this whole island, and when I'm done with you—"

His cell phone rang, and he held up one finger, politely, as if he was simply dying to hear the rest of what she had to say.

"Yes, sir. Of course I'm with her. We're leaving the airport now, and coming back to the palace."

So much for the rest of what she had to say! Jordan bit her lip and glared angrily at the man. He was irritatingly unintimidated.

"Where's the elephant?" Whitney cried, stamping her foot.

"Shush, dear." Jordan took a deep steadying breath. Much as she wanted to make a scene, her first obligation was to keep calm for her daughter. She didn't want Whitney frightened by all this. "We'll have to see the elephant another day."

"Why?" Whitney shrieked.

"Because of this gentleman right here," Jordan said.

Whitney scowled up at the remote featured Mr. Webster, wound up, and kicked him soundly in the shin.

He winced, but was quite manly about it.

"Can I go back to Tubby?" Whitney asked her mother, her rage vented.

"He's no replacement for a real, live elephant, but I suppose we have no option," Jordan said.

Webster gestured for them to precede him out of the airport, and Jordan went, chin up to try and hide the fact she felt like a prisoner. Outside the airport were three secret service cars and half a dozen agents. She tossed one of them the keys to the Mini. "See this gets back to Ralph Miller."

And then she slid into the back seat of a long gray car, while Webster held open the door. She took her daughter on her lap, and Webster got in the seat beside her looking very stern and ready to grab her should she try and leap from the vehicle.

The prince was waiting in the driveway looking firm and formidable, not at all like the fun-loving boy who had been kissing her toes this morning.

Big surprise that *that* wasn't who he really was.

She exited the car regally.

"Hewo Pwince Owen. My mommy was going to take me to see an elephant. That awful man stopped us."

Jordan glanced at the "awful man" and saw he was looking at his shoes. Owen didn't even try to hide his fury. His eyes were snapping with it, the line of his jaw was leaping.

"I'll take you to see an elephant another time," Owen said.

"Over my dead body," Jordan spat back.

To her disgrace, it was Owen who cast a look at their daughter, who was watching them with worried eyes.

He signaled to Trisha who swooped forward and claimed Whitney.

"Where's she taking her?" Jordan asked, and saw his brow furrow at the fear in her voice.

"To get her ready to have lunch with my mother, which is where you're supposed to be, too."

"I don't recall being invited," she said snootily.

"You were so invited. I found my mother's invitation, unopened, in your room when I went to find you after Ralph sought me out to tell me some remarkable tale about you being fired if you didn't find mushrooms. I hate mushrooms. I doubt they'd be on the menu for my celebration."

"Your mother did invite me for lunch? Not just Whitney?"

"Why would she just invite Whitney?"

"Don't play the innocent with me, Owen. Others might fall for you hook, line and sinker, but I've seen your other side."

"I'm not following you. Even a little bit."

"I heard you! I heard you telling your sister you wanted Whitney. I heard her saying her mother was never going to let her go now that she knew about her." Don't cry, she ordered herself. Don't you dare cry.

Of course, she started to cry.

"Oh, Jordan," he said and put his arms around her.

"Don't touch me," she said, then traitorously snuggled deeper into his embrace. Why did her heart think it knew things that her head could not accept?

That some men—that this man—was someone she could trust.

Forever.

"You heard part of a very long conversation. I would never take Whitney away from you. Never. Nor would I allow anybody else to."

"So you'll keep me here, against my will, just to keep Whitney."

"I won't keep you here against your will."

"You already have," she reminded him tartly, but still didn't pull out of his arms like a stronger, saner woman would have done.

"Your security team has standing orders. They are for your protection."

"My security team?" she echoed. "I have a security team?"

"Yes. Webster heads it. He's one of my most trusted men."

"Why would I have a security team?"

"Even before your name was publicly linked with mine in the paper, the people who kidnapped me knew your name and expressed interest in you. That made you vulnerable in ways you never were before."

"How could they have known my name?" she said.

He looked away, embarrassed. He said, very softly, "When I was their prisoner, I called it in my sleep."

She stared at him. Could he be making this up? He looked too thoroughly embarrassed to have made it up. He had called her in his sleep!

She could feel the defenses crumbling again. She hated it that he had this effect on her. Hated it.

"Is Whitney safe?" she asked, with new fear. "From kidnappers?"

"Of course she is. Both of you have been under intense security."

"But how could I not know that?"

"A good security team can be nearly invisible if they have to be."

She was falling for it. It all seemed so plausible. She *wanted* to believe him. But she couldn't. Mustn't. "Be that as it may, I still know what I heard you say to your sister."

"Look, we're late for lunch with my mother. No one keeps the queen waiting. After lunch we'll talk about what you think you heard. If you still want to leave," he shrugged, almost carelessly, "I won't try to stop you."

Irrationally, she felt annoyed at how easily he was going to give her up. "I'm not going for lunch with your mother."

He smiled, just a touch testily. "Jordan, you can say no to me, but nobody says no to a summons from the queen."

It was tempting to be the first, but the truth was, curiosity overtook her. The truth was she felt suddenly too tired to fight.

The truth was he had called her name in his sleep.

At least that sounded like the truth.

An hour later, dressed in her best black slack suit Jordan, Owen and Whitney were ushered into the palace dining room. Whitney had a ribbon in her hair, and was wearing an adorable white dress that did not possibly look like it could survive lunch with a four-year-old. Owen was in pressed slacks, a shirt, a pullover sweater.

He looked every ounce the prince that he was.

Queen Marissa made a terrible fuss over Whitney and Whitney lapped up every ounce of it. Jordan, tired and cranky, only just managed to be polite.

But the queen seemed to take everybody by surprise when lunch was over and she said to Owen, "Son, why don't you take Whitney down to the kennel? I heard there was a new litter of puppies there."

Owen looked surprised, but after a quick glance at his mother gave no argument.

Jordan waited in silence after they had gone. She wanted to dislike the queen, but found she could not. The woman was gracious and dignified and personable. There was a softness in her eyes that was most compelling.

"I want to thank you for your work at the mine yesterday, Ms. Ashbury. Or may I call you Jordan?" At Jordan's nod, she went on. "I heard how you worked in the canteen, did practical things to bring comfort."

"Do you hear everything?" Jordan asked.

The queen smiled. "Just about."

"Then do you know I tried to leave the island this morning?"

"Yes. Would you like to tell me why?"

So she told her about the part of the conversation she had heard Owen have with Anastasia.

"Oh, my dear, how dreadful for you to think we would steal your daughter from you! It's completely untrue, of course. You must have only heard part of a more complicated conversation."

How could you not believe a woman who possessed this much grace, and whose eyes were lit from within with character and strength?

"It's true, I would like to be a part of my granddaughter's life,'' the queen said quietly. ''Would I keep you here against your will to make that happen? No.''

Jordan sighed. ''I don't know what to believe anymore.''

''The truth is you haven't known what to believe since he left you five years ago, isn't that true?''

She looked at the woman startled.

''Trust shattered is the hardest thing to repair,'' the queen said. ''I know that. My brother was murdered many years ago. It changed who I was, just as Owen leaving you alone changed who you are.''

''Yes.'' It felt like no one had understood that before.

''At the risk of sounding trite, I have found dark clouds do have silver linings. My loss taught me to appreciate what I have while I have it.''

''I suppose I learned things, too,'' Jordan said reluctantly. ''I just don't know what.''

The queen smiled. ''In a time when everyone puts themselves first, Jordan, you learned to be selfless. You learned to put another first, your daughter. And I understand you've used the experiences of your own life to help other young mothers. To me, this is the greatest test of character—can we use what life hands us to become better and stronger and wiser instead of bitter and cynical and self-protective?''

Jordan thought, not without shame, that she had been bitter and cynical and self-protective with Owen. So much so, that perhaps it was that—her own attitude—that had sent her running for home, not the words she had overheard.

''I think I'm afraid of loving him,'' she said out loud, and then blushed wildly. She had just told the queen of Penwyck she was in love!

And the queen was smiling gently at her, as if that was not such terrible news.

The queen said, "Perhaps I could share something with you that life has taught me?"

"Please."

"We use this word called love because it is convenient, but really I have found love encompasses many feelings and emotions. It is part passion and part exhilaration and part hope and part wonder. Love has so many elements, but as the years go by, I find one element of love stands apart from all the others."

Jordan found herself holding her breath, as if the secret to the universe was about to be revealed to her.

"And that part," the queen said softly, "is forgiveness. You see, the initial stages of love lead us to believe the one we love is perfect, but who in this world is perfect? And so as the years go by that illusion of perfection is replaced by something more real. We find our loved ones, far from belonging on the pedestals we have placed them on, have foibles and weaknesses.

"To truly love," she continued softly, "is to see all of a person, to forgive them their imperfections, their humanity. It is the quality of forgiveness that lifts love up to the next plane, where we no longer love an illusion that fulfilled some need in us, but rather we love someone who is real, who we can give something to, rather than take from.

"To me, it is as if love grows up, leaves its childish illusions behind it, and becomes real. Many years ago in California," the queen said gently, "you fell in love with a man who became your prince, a fairy-tale love. Now, the question is, can you love a prince into becoming your man?"

"That's why I want to go home," Jordan confessed.

"I feel too confused here, as if I will never find the answer."

"You are free to go home if you wish," the queen said. "Please just notify me so that I can make the proper security arrangements for you. But if I may say something? I have rarely found myself able to solve a problem by running away from it. Mind you, I have rarely found an answer by running after it, either. The harder I chase, the further it gets from my grasp."

"Then what?"

"Why don't you just wait," the queen said. "And let the answer find you?"

"And if it doesn't?"

"But it will."

"I believe you," Jordan said. "I know it's probably improper to say this, but I feel as if I have known you for a very long time, and as though I can trust you."

The queen looked troubled. "I am honored by that, my dear, though my failings are also many, and I too must count on forgiveness being an element of love in the near future."

Owen was waiting for her when Jordan finally came out of the dining area. "That was quite the lengthy lunch. What did you talk about?"

"Where's my daughter? You're supposed to be looking after her."

"She's having her nap. What on earth did you and my mother talk about for so long?"

"Do you think I would have nothing to say to a queen?"

"Has anybody ever told you a porcupine has less prickles than you?"

"That would have been you. On our second date. Murphy's Pub and Pizzeria. We had pepperoni and draught beer. Your mother, on the other hand, seemed to find me quite charming. She told me I could go home if I wanted to. That she would help me make the arrangements herself.'' She recognized she was trying to goad him, make him plead with her to stay.

''She what?'' He did sound annoyed.

''You heard me.''

''Jordan, you're being unreasonable.''

Now that she knew she loved him, he was supposed to get down on one knee and confess his love for her, beg her to stay! No, instead, a porcupine had less prickles.

''Stay until my celebration,'' he suggested, his voice cool. ''It's only one more day away. If you want to go after that, I won't try to stop you. I promise.''

''Oh, the oath thing.'' Wouldn't try to stop her? That wasn't how the script went. The prince was supposed to track her to the ends of the earth, glass slipper in hand.

''You know, you are difficult, impossible and preposterous. I can't think why on earth, with all the women to choose from, I'm so in love with you.''

She stared at him, open-mouthed, as he stalked away from her down the hallway.

I'm so in love with you, sang in her head. ''I guess if you want me to stay that badly,'' she called after him, ''I could. Just for the ball.''

''On second thought,'' he called over his shoulder, ''don't bother.''

Oh! Don't bother? Wild horses couldn't keep her away from that celebration now! She would show him a thing or two! He was going to be sorry he had called her difficult. Impossible! Preposterous! And unreasonable!

She was going to show up at his celebration, and she

was going to be so beautiful he wouldn't be able to think of anything else.

Every name he had called her would be shoved from his brain.

Any doubt that he ever had that she would not fit perfectly into his world would be washed away.

She was going to make Prince Owen Michael Penwyck sorry he had ever messed with her. He was going to be the sorriest man in the world that he had ever walked away.

She stopped herself.

Who was she trying to kid? She had never been that kind of woman. She had never been a showstopper, never once in her whole life turned a head.

She might as well go and pack her bags and leave Penwyck now.

She found her way back to her room. And sitting in the middle of her bed was a huge box. She opened it, and when she saw what was inside, tears came to her eyes.

For she knew she was going to the ball, after all.

"With my luck," she muttered, "at the stroke of midnight, it will be all over, just like it was for Cinderella. Not that I've ever cared for Cinderella, a childishly dependent fool who waited for a prince to solve her problems for her."

Still, she picked up the dress, a dress made of froth and dreams and nothing else, and hugged it to herself and knew she was going to the ball.

Chapter Nine

"Dinner is exquisite, don't you think, Owen?"

"Exquisite," he muttered, to his sister Anastasia. The truth was he might as well be eating cardboard for all that he had noticed the taste of the meal in front of him. He had noticed, abstractly, that the food looked rather odd, but since Jordan had walked in the room, it was as if his every sense was locked on her. Those senses that weren't needed to look at her seemed to have shut down, sending all their energy to the ones that were.

Which might explain why it felt as if scales had fallen from his eyes, as if he had been blind, but now could see. He had never seen a woman so utterly and breathtakingly gorgeous!

The gown, that had looked so innocent in its box, fit her beautifully. Made of what appeared to be antique ivory silk, there was nothing old-fashioned about the fit of that dress. It slid sensuously around her curves, accentuating the ultrafeminine swell of breast and hip. It made her every move seem like a siren song.

The dress had obviously been a big mistake on his part. Before, when her beauty had seemed more inward than outward, he'd been the only man who knew how beautiful she was. Now, he could see every man in the room had her on radar, just as he did, aware of her every movement, tracking it, all the while trying to appear not to be the least bit interested in her!

And it wasn't just the dress, or the grace that she wore it with, as if she'd been born to wear such things.

Tonight she had her hair pulled back into a tight bun, and it might have looked severe, except that the hair that hugged the lovely shape of her head was so glossy that he knew that there was not a man in the room who was not picturing himself pulling the pins out of it, watching it cascade down toward round, soft shoulders, running his fingers through the silk of it. He was probably the only man here who knew that hairstyle was some sort of illusion, a feminine trick. She didn't have enough hair to pull it back like that, to have it in a bun.

When had Jordan become versed in feminine wiles? It was a frightening thought. She was far too smart already! If she started directing all that intelligence at attracting male attention, hope for his half of the species was over.

Still, whatever she was doing was working, because he commanded himself not to be sucked in to her new-found power, to look away, but he could not. Instead he found himself analyzing how the hairstyle showed off bone structure that amazed him. When had she developed those kind of cheekbones? How had she made her eyes look so huge and so blue? Had her mouth always looked that sensuous, that wide, that kissable? Had her mouth always looked like it tasted good?

And then, she leaned forward to talk to someone—a

man, of course, at her end of the table, and his focus was once again on the dress.

What kind of engineering marvel was keeping everything in? And she did not have breasts like that! She didn't. He had just seen her in a bathing suit and her figure was delightful to be sure, but this? If he had noticed the dress had this kind of neckline when it was in the box, it would still be in the box! The straight line had looked so innocent!

Who could have guessed the upper portion of her was going to be on display, the creamy swell of flawless skin showing so tantalizingly, round, full—

"What part do you like the best?" his sister asked.

Of Jordan? He avoided looking at his sister, thinking he had probably been caught staring inappropriately at Jordan's cleavage. That would probably be tomorrow's headline. Pervert Prince Eyes Decollete.

"Owen," his sister said, rolling her eyes, "really! I meant the meal."

There was a smile in her eyes and he suspected she knew darn well he wasn't tasting a thing on his plate.

"This," he said, trying to fool her, touching something with his fork that looked like seaweed topped with flowers. Were those nasturtiums forming that colorful orange banner across his plate? Were they the very nasturtiums he had used to barter an afternoon with Jordan? What a lot of good they had done him!

"I loved that, too," Anastasia said, "What would you call that flavor. Smoky?"

Jordan's eyes were smoky. The flavor was… interesting. "Delicious," he said with not an ounce of sincerity.

His sister laughed. "And what do you think of the

beef? I understand the sauce was prepared with velvet from the antler of a moose.''

Oh, shut up—can't you see I'm preoccupied? He hated it that he had involved his sister in his life by borrowing that gown from her. Next thing he'd known, Anastasia and Jordan had been hanging out together. He was sure it was Anastasia leading Jordan astray, showing her all those tricks with makeup and decollete.

All day, the pair of them had been acting like school-girls, Jordan acting as if she didn't have a care in the world, instead of like a woman with a major decision to make.

Stay or go.

So far, his mother was going to help Jordan get home if she decided to go, and his sister was going to be her best buddy. Instead of him.

Not that he was thinking anything like buddy thoughts every time he glanced down the table and saw her. In that dress. He picked the tinkle of her laughter out of the sounds around him, and thought he should leave here. He would love to go and change out of this stiff formal wear. He hated it anyway, the white collar, heavily starched, chafed at the bottom of his jaw. The tailed black jacket looked pompous, the royal medallion pinned so precisely on his chest made him look like a general in some wildly warm jungle nation. He disliked cummerbunds and gloves and bow ties.

He was going to be king, and he hated pomp and circumstance.

He closed his eyes and imagined himself anywhere but here. He would like to be in the stables, surrounded by the rich, ripe real smells of the place. He thought of brushing the coat of his big Friesian gelding until it gleamed blacker than coal. He could see himself putting on the saddle, tugging the girth tight, turning the stirrup, and leaping on in one smooth motion.

He ordered his mind to take him down forest paths bathed in moonlight, but his mind rebelled. In his imagination, instead of riding into the inviting silence of the forest, he was riding toward the palace. Right up the stairs and into the ballroom, delighting in scattered people and tables. He swooped her up, covered her protesting mouth with his, whirled the horse and—

"Oh, look," Anastasia said, "there's Ralph and Trisha. Don't they look lovely? Owen, it was so sweet of you to ask them to come."

He opened his eyes and looked where his sister gestured and then wished he hadn't. His mother's tradition was that palace staff were to be treated as members of their extended family. They were to be included in functions whenever possible, so given that Ralph's romance seemed to be progressing quite a bit better than his own, and to reward his loyalty in reporting Jordan's escape attempt, Owen had invited him to bring his girl to the ball.

The young couple looked blissfully happy, Ralph as unaware of what he was eating as Owen was, and for a completely different reason. Trisha was focused so intently on Ralph, smiling up at him. As Owen watched, she hesitated, looked around and then mischievously popped a pickle into Ralph's mouth. At a royal banquet!

Owen looked swiftly away. That's what Jordan should be doing! Smiling at him and flouting convention, as always, by popping pickles into his mouth.

But oh, no, Jordan was sitting halfway across the room looking absolutely fascinated by Peter Webster, looking like she had been born to settings like this one, and not flouting convention at all.

Owen frowned. Was Webster the type women thought of as good-looking? He felt he was seeing the man's solid build, his square jaw and blond hair for the first time. Bodyguards and the women they protected had long histories of the forced intimacy of that relationship crossing boundaries.

"Can you tell me why she isn't sitting beside me?" he asked Anastasia. The question required him to swallow his pride. Jordan had tried to escape from him! She had acted as if he was capable of the most despicable kind of behavior! Okay, maybe her believing that was not completely out of line, but how long did she expect him to wear sackcloth and ashes over it? How long until she forgave him?

He frowned suddenly. It occurred to him that he had never asked her to forgive him.

"Why who isn't sitting beside you?" Anastasia said innocently.

"You know darn well who. Quit toying with me."

"Or what? Off to the dungeon?"

"She's been giving you lessons in snippy repartee, I see."

His sister didn't ask who this time. "If you don't enjoy her conversation, I can't see why you'd disapprove of her sitting over there. Mr. Webster looks like he is thoroughly enjoying her company."

He felt like his teeth were going to be ground to dust before the evening was through. Had everyone forgotten this celebration was supposed to be about him?

"Who said one word about disapproval? I asked a simple question. Why is she sitting over there? With Peter Webster?"

"Oh, Jordan and I played around with the seating plan

a bit. So much more interesting when you sit beside someone you don't know.''

He could point out that he was seated beside her, his own sister, whom he knew quite a bit better than he wanted to at the moment. Or he could point out that Ralph knew Trisha, but he had the feeling that he would only be rising to the bait.

''Did she request a seat beside Peter?'' he heard himself asking, despite the order he had just given himself to not say one more word about Jordan Ashbury.

His sister glanced over at Jordan, and smiled as if Jordan's obvious enjoyment of the evening was her own personal triumph. ''I don't think so. Just a coincidence, I'm sure.''

How sure? ''You've been cozy with Jordan today.'' He tried not to make it an accusation and failed miserably.

''I thought, given your interest in her, the fact she is the mother of my only niece, I should get to know her. She is so much fun!''

Jordan fun? She was about as much fun as playing in a tubful of tacks! So why did he feel he could no longer live without her?

Because he had always seen the softness she tried to disguise with those sharp edges. He had always been able to coax the fun side out of her. Was he mildly annoyed that she had showed that side of herself to his sister so rapidly when he had to work so hard to get to that place in her?

''I took her horseback riding this afternoon. She's a natural.''

''Jordan? On a horse? What are you doing? You could have killed her!'' The fierceness of his instinct to protect caught even him off guard.

"Nonsense. I teach riding to disabled children, for heaven's sake. The horse was only slightly bigger than Tubby and not nearly as energetic. You know that little Fjord gelding that we received as a gift from Norway?"

"Why would you take her horseback riding?" he asked. "She never expressed the slightest desire to go with me."

"Did you ever give her a chance to express her desires? Or were you too busy expressing your own?"

He looked at Anastasia narrowly. How much information had the two young women been exchanging? Did his sister put just the slightest emphasis on the word desire, as if she knew things about him that he considered intensely private? Like how much he enjoyed kissing Jordan's toes?

Not that what she said was completely untrue. He'd done a lot of talking to Jordan about what he wanted. How much had he asked about what she wanted?

"Because she told me," his sister said sweetly, "she doesn't want to ride on the back of a horse, like some fainting flower who could be swept off her feet by a man. She wants to ride her own horse through life. I think those were her words. I say bully for her."

"As if she could ever be a fainting flower," he grumbled, and nixed the horse into the ballroom plan. If he couldn't sweep her off her feet, what the hell was he supposed to do?

Dessert came. He stared at it glumly. Jell-O at a royal banquet. Not plain Jell-O. It looked like it had fall leaves set in it. He could not even pretend interest in it.

The dishes were, finally, mercifully cleared away. He entertained the possibility he might get through this evening.

But then the band began warming up their instruments. There was going to be dancing soon. He was not going to get through this evening if he had to watch her dance with Peter Webster!

"Would you have the first dance with me, brother dearest?"

"No."

He got up swiftly, and wound his way to Jordan. There was this thing left undone between them. These words left unsaid. He stood there for a moment, and when she didn't look up, he touched her shoulder.

A mistake. It was softer than silk, familiar. It reminded him of touching her shoulder in other times, all he had walked away from, all he had lost.

"Would you dance with me, Jordan?" Those weren't the words he intended at all.

And yet somehow they were the right ones, because when she looked up at him, he saw she was pleased to be asked. Still, she hesitated.

Cinderella was not supposed to reject the prince! That was not in the script. His script. How did her script read?

Then she put her hand in his, and he suspected, not without pleasure, that she was as powerless over these forces that swirled around them as he was.

Her hand was small and lovely, and yet strong. It fit perfectly into the curve of his. He bent over it, very formally, and kissed it, and then drew her to him, led her to the very center of the empty floor.

This was one thing they had never done together. They had never danced. The music started and they were alone in the middle of the huge polished ball room floor. He bowed to her.

She curtsied.

His hand found hers again and he drew her to him. He had danced formally all his life. He had begun ballroom dancing lessons almost as soon as he had learned to walk. It was part of what he did, part of his duty as a prince. He had opened more dances this way than he cared to think about.

But never once had it been like this. Dancing with Jordan was not a duty. Not in the least. Dancing with her was magic.

Pure and undiluted magic.

Never before had his eyes locked with another's like this, never before had he felt the subtle pull of energy shivering in the air between two bodies. He drew her a little closer, put his hand on the small of her back and felt the warmth, the mystical force of her radiating to him.

He felt her find his rhythm at the exact moment he found hers.

They didn't dance, so much as they floated. Mortals danced. They became something more. Winged. Free. They had found their way to a place beyond words, beyond misunderstandings, beyond human failings and frailties. Finally, they had found their way.

Everything that had passed before this moment in time faded to utter insignificance. Everything that would come after was illuminated in a soft light, the future and all its promise dancing with them.

Love shimmered and played in the air around them. It soared on wings made stronger for the fact they had been singed.

Owen became aware of an odd quality of silence in the ballroom. Always, above the strains of the music were other sounds: chatter, laughter, waiters clinking glasses, chairs being shuffled. He was not sure he had ever heard an opening dance this silent. The music, the sound of her gown swishing across the floor and their hearts beating. Nothing more.

They swept around the floor, her following his lead perfectly, effortlessly, gracefully, and it was as if the world belonged to just the two of them. Finally, they were perfectly in step, perfectly in tune.

The music of the first dance ended, and after a long space, far away he heard the sound of applause, but even that did not come into his world.

The words poured back, the words his soul needed to speak.

"I needed to ask you something," he said, his mouth near her ear, smelling the sweet smell at the curve of her neck.

She pulled back from him slightly, scanned his face.

His voice caught in his throat. "I need to ask you two things," he corrected himself.

She nodded. He could feel she had stopped breathing against him.

"I need," he whispered in her ear, "to ask your forgiveness."

She stood very still. She looked straight into his eyes. He could see every pain he had ever caused her there, and for a moment her pain felt like it would rip out his very heart.

And then the miracle happened. She reached up, and touched his cheek with the palm of her hand, and it was a gesture of such exquisite tenderness. And as she looked at him, the pain faded from her eyes and was replaced with a lustrous and miraculous light that was like nothing he had ever seen, ever. The stars coming out would be shamed by it, the sun in the morning was not so pure as was the light in her eyes.

A single tear trickled down her cheek.

"Of course I forgive you, Owen," she said, her voice raspy with emotion. And then she smiled, radiant, tried to wipe away the tear. He caught her hand, and kissed the tear from her cheek.

It tasted pure and sweet and free of bitterness.

"And the second question," he said huskily—

"Your attention, please. Everyone. Your attention."

Annoyed at this interruption to the most important moment of his entire life, Owen had no option but to turn to the podium. Her hand slipped into his and her shoulder rested against his chest.

"Prince Broderick of Penwyck."

The crowd clapped politely, but Owen eyed his uncle warily. Broderick seemed to be delighting in all the pomp and circumstance. Like his nephew, he was dressed very formally. Owen noted his uncle looked unusually happy.

Or on closer inspection, perhaps happy was the wrong word, but definitely pleased with himself. Sly. Smug.

Owen shot a look at his mother. She, too, looked on guard as Broderick took the microphone.

"Good evening, ladies and gentlemen," Broderick said, "and especially a good evening to you, Your Royal Highness Prince Owen, whose safe return from peril is the cause for this celebration tonight."

Owen acknowledged his uncle's bow with a slight inclination of his head.

"I wanted to take this opportunity to commend our Royal Elite Team," Broderick went on smoothly, "for their quick action in finding our prince and returning him, unharmed and safely to us."

The applause was deafening.

Broderick held up his hands, obviously enjoying the limelight.

Owen wished he did not feel such dislike for his uncle. It was the system that had created this man. And if he and Dylan were not careful, the same system would do this to one of them.

"Naturally," Broderick said sadly, "a nation holds its breath when the heir apparent goes missing."

He cleared his throat, shook off the sadness with dramatic flair, and smiled. "But what if it wasn't really the heir apparent who had gone missing?"

All chatter ceased, every rustling of gowns, every clinking of glasses, and then a whisper of confusion swelled within the crowd.

"I have a confession to make," Broderick said, and Owen felt his unease grow.

What on earth was his uncle up to?

"Twenty-three years ago, twins were born to our wonderful king, Morgan, my brother, and his beautiful wife, Marissa. But it was me, always cognizant of the danger surrounding heirs to the throne, who thought perhaps I could serve my country best by putting the new princes out of harm's way."

Owen felt mesmerized, as if he was watching a snake being charmed out of a basket. He was able to pull his eyes away from Broderick only long enough to look at his mother.

She looked very pale.

Broderick's smile deepened, and he dropped his bombshell. "I switched the twins at birth."

A gasp went up from the crowd. Owen might have laughed at his uncle's absurdity had he not seen the effect Broderick's words had on his mother. Owen was not sure he had ever seen her look anything but composed. At the moment, Queen Marissa looked distinctly shaken.

''The true heir to the throne, will not be our Prince Owen, who is in fact, by birth not a prince at all, as all of Penwyck has believed. Nor will our future king be his happily wandering brother, Dylan.''

By birth not a prince at all. Owen registered the words, but felt oddly unmoved by them.

''The true heir to the throne of Penwyck will indeed be one of Morgan and Marissa's twin sons, but not the boys we have watched grow to young manhood. The true heirs to Penwyck were raised, thanks to me, in complete safety and comfort by a very wealthy family in America.''

For a moment, there was stunned silence, and then the hall dissolved into chaos, as people all began to talk at once.

Owen felt Jordan's fingers dig into his arm where she had been holding him. He glanced down at her, and saw her eyes wide on his face, disbelieving. He scanned her features, and a small smile tugged at his lips.

She was worried, not that he might not be a prince, but about him and how he might be reacting to not being a prince.

He, on the other hand, was worried about his mother. Or the woman he had always thought was his mother. Perhaps only he would have noticed how she flinched back from Broderick's words, but already he could see she was composing herself.

She got to her feet, regal and serene, and as soon as she stood, silence once again fell over the hall. She looked every inch the queen, tall and imperious. She wore a small and tasteful tiara tonight, and a brocaded gown.

Every eye was on her as she made her way gracefully to the microphone. She didn't walk to it, she swept to it, the most powerful woman in Penwyck. Broderick was dwarfed by her power and he seemed to know it, shrinking back from the microphone.

"My dearest brother-in-law," she said with great and grave dignity, "I would fear you had been in the sun too long, but since the hot days of summer are over, perhaps it is the influence of those soap operas you like to while away your afternoons watching that have caused you to make this very strange and very disturbing announcement."

A nervous laugh swept the hall, and Broderick's color became very unbecoming as Marissa looked at him steadily, until finally he looked away.

Owen was far less interested in Broderick than the queen. Ah, she was handling herself beautifully, as always, but still he could tell something in Broderick's announcement had touched a nerve in her that she was being very careful not to let others see.

"Though I have no doubt," she said, her voice smooth and soothing and unperturbed, "that one of the sons I have raised will one day wear the crown of his father—"

Again, Owen heard what others might not hear. His mother had not named him as the certain successor to his father. Her eyes met his, held and then skittered away, and he was sure he had not misinterpreted her action.

"—I will, of course, investigate this claim that Broderick has made, just as I would any that was so disruptive to our family and indeed to all the people of Penwyck. I will have a special meeting of the Royal Elite Team tonight, and we will decide on a course of action. I'm sure, that within weeks, I will be able to confirm, with proof, who the heirs to the throne of Penwyck really are.

"Naturally, Prince Broderick," the queen looked over her shoulder at her brother-in-law, but still addressed the crowd, "I would have much preferred you bring such a serious matter to me privately, but I understand we each have our own style of dealing with things."

Her reprimand, her implication that Broderick's handling of this sensitive matter had been tasteless and crass caused another nervous little twitter of laughter to sweep the crowd.

Broderick looked absolutely apoplectic, his face flushed, his features twisted into a fury that reminded Owen that his uncle could be dangerous.

The tension in the room was now palpable. Owen could see enormous damage was going to be done to Penwyck if people were allowed to leave the ball on this note. Rumors would spread. Gossip would catch fire. It would be as if the monarchy, the leadership, of the country was unstable.

Broderick had done a great deal of damage in a few short seconds. The entire economy of the country could be pulled down if too much credence was given to the startling announcements of this evening.

Patting Jordan's arm, Owen pulled away from her, and made his way quickly through the crowd. The crowd parted before him, and he sensed the anxiety in the room, the need for leadership.

Owen leapt onto the stage from the floor.

He bowed to his mother, extended his hand to Broderick, though there was no missing the reluctance with which he accepted it, nor the malice in his eyes.

And then he turned to the crowd, and looked at their worried faces. He smiled, and he felt the energy in the room shift imperceptibly. He held the smile, met eyes, was rewarded when people smiled back.

Then he took the microphone.

Keeping his tone deliberately light, he said, "I wasn't told this would be a surprise party, but thank you, Broderick, that was quite a surprise."

A ripple of appreciative laughter followed this statement.

"My mother has promised to get to the bottom of this," Owen continued, "and we all know my mother. We can place our absolute faith in her to untangle this web, as we have placed our absolute faith in her so many other times here on Penwyck."

He had come to stand right beside her right shoulder, presenting a united front. He met her eyes. Her mouth was smiling, but her eyes were pleading. For what?

Perhaps it was because he had just made its acquaintance so recently that he recognized it so readily. Forgiveness.

He had a feeling this might not end the way anyone thought it was going to. But tonight his only public duty was damage control.

And of course his very private one was to ask Jordan the second question.

"My understanding," Owen said, "was that this was a party celebrating my safe return." He paused, and looked at each of his limbs slowly, patted his chest, and said, "As I thought, I am still safely returned!"

The laughter was relieved now.

"So let the band strike up, and let us dance and celebrate. Tomorrow is soon enough to deal with the problems of the world."

He signaled the band leader, who immediately struck up an upbeat tune. He blessed his sisters for knowing exactly what to do. They tugged partners onto the dance floor, and in moments the whole floor was crowded with people.

He made his way through them, and bowed to Jordan, who was looking at him with sparkling eyes.

"Have I told you recently, that I think you are magnificent?" she asked him.

"Recently? You've never told me that."

"Oh, but I have."

He actually felt himself blush. "I have a second question to ask you," he said. The music stopped.

He noticed the crowd was still restive, and he held up his hand. With no microphone this time, he asked for the attention of the crowd and got it.

"I need to say something else tonight and it is this— kings and queens and princes and princesses come, and they go. Kingdoms rise and then they fade. All my life I have been obedient to my duty, and to you, the people of Penwyck.

"But tonight I am also going to be obedient to my heart. Over time, and history will bear me out on this, only one thing remains.

"And that is love."

He faced Jordan. She had her hands up, framing her lovely face. Her eyes were wide. He took her hand, and then he dropped on one knee before her. He looked up at her, into her eyes, and in front of all these witnesses, he proclaimed himself.

He said, "Jordan Ashbury you are my world. I do not know what the future holds, nor does any man, though we sometimes allow ourselves that illusion.

"If you are not at my side I could be a king, but without you I would be poorer than any pauper.

"But if you say yes to spending your life at my side,

I could well be a pauper, but I will feel richer than the richest of kings.

"Jordan, will you walk through the days of my life at my side? Will you put your hand in mine? Will you allow me the great privilege of being the father to all your children? Jordan Ashbury, will you be my wife?"

She tugged at his hands, and he stood, and looking down at her, he saw the answer in her eyes before she spoke the word.

A single word.

The word was yes.

"I don't know about anyone else's," she whispered, "but my prince has been found!"

* * * * *

Join the Penwycks as they unravel
the scandal surrounding the kingdom when
CROWN & GLORY
continues next month
in Silhouette Romance with
THE PRINCESS HAS AMNESIA!
by Patricia Thayer (SR #1606).

**Where royalty and romance
go hand in hand...**

The series continues in Silhouette Romance
with these unforgettable novels:

HER ROYAL HUSBAND
by Cara Colter
on sale July 2002 (SR #1600)

THE PRINCESS HAS AMNESIA!
by Patricia Thayer
on sale August 2002 (SR #1606)

SEARCHING FOR HER PRINCE
by Karen Rose Smith
on sale September 2002 (SR #1612)

And look for more Crown and Glory stories in
SILHOUETTE DESIRE starting in October 2002!

Available at your favorite retail outlet.

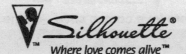

If you enjoyed what you just read,
then we've got an offer you can't resist!

Take 2 bestselling love stories FREE!

Plus get a FREE surprise gift!

COMING NEXT MONTH

#1606 THE PRINCESS HAS AMNESIA!—Patricia Thayer
Crown and Glory
Who was the beauty that fell from the sky—right into former FBI agent Jake Sanderstone's mountain refuge? Ana was bossy, stricken with amnesia and...a princess! But when her memory came flooding back, would she let go of love and return to royalty?

#1607 FALLING FOR THE SHEIK—Carol Grace
A bad fall at a ski run left Rahman Harun helpless—and he hated it. But when private nurse Amanda Reston entered his family's cabin, the strong sheik decided he needed her tender, loving care! Her nurturing nature healed his body. Could she also heal his wounded heart?

#1608 IN DEEP WATERS—Melissa McClone
A Tale of the Sea
Kai Waterton had been warned to stay away from the sea. That didn't stop her from heading an expedition to find a sunken ship—or falling for single dad and salvager Ben Mendoza! But what would happen to their budding romance when the mysteries of her past were uncovered...?

#1609 THE LAST VIRGIN IN OAKDALE—Wendy Warren
Be Eleanor's "love tutor"? Cole Sullivan was shocked. His once-shy buddy in high school, now a tenderhearted veterinarian, had chosen her former crush to initiate her in the art of lovemaking. But Cole found himself with second thoughts...and third thoughts...all about Eleanor!

#1610 BOUGHT BY THE BILLIONAIRE—Myrna Mackenzie
The Wedding Auction
When Maggie Todd entered herself in a charity auction, she'd never anticipated being asked to pretend to be royalty! As the wealthy charmer Ethan Bennington tutored the unsophisticated yet enticing Maggie in becoming a "lady," he found he wanted her to become *his* lady....

#1611 FIRST YOU KISS 100 MEN...—Carolyn Greene
Being the Mystery Kisser was easy for columnist Julie Fasano—at first. Anonymously writing about kissing men got more difficult when she met up with investigator Hunter Matthews. Hunter was determined to find the kisser's identity—would he discover her little secret as *they* shared kisses?